THIS DIARY BELONGS TO:

Nikki J. Maxwell

PRIVATE & CONFIDENTIAL

If found, please return to ME for REWARD!

(NO SNOOPING ALLOWED!!!☹)

ALSO BY *Rachel Renée Russell*

DORK DIARIES

THE MISADVENTURES OF MAX CRUMBLY

Rachel Renée Russell

Double

DORK

diaries

with Nikki Russell and Erin Russell

SIMON & SCHUSTER

First published as an omnibus edition in Great Britain in 2020 by Simon & Schuster UK Ltd

Simon & Schuster UK Ltd
1st Floor, 222 Gray's Inn Road, London WC1X 8HB

Dork Diaries: Frenemies Forever first published in Great Britain in 2016 by Simon & Schuster UK Ltd.
Originally published in 2016 in the USA as Dork Diaries 11: Tales from a Not-so-friendly Frenemy
by Aladdin, an imprint of Simon & Schuster Children's Publishing Division.

Dork Diaries: Crush Catastrophe first published in Great Britain in 2017 by Simon & Schuster UK Ltd.
Originally published in 2017 in the USA as Dork Diaries 12: Tales from a Not-so-secret Crush Catastrophe
by Aladdin, an imprint of Simon & Schuster Children's Publishing Division.

1 3 5 7 9 10 8 6 4 2

www.simonandschuster.co.uk
www.simonandschuster.com.au
www.simonandschuster.co.in

Simon & Schuster Australia, Sydney
Simon & Schuster India, New Delhi

A CIP catalogue record for this book is available from the British Library.

ISBN 978-1-4711-9691-1
eBook ISBN 978-1-4711-9692-8

Printed and bound in India by Replika Press Pvt. Ltd.

MIX
Paper from
responsible sources
FSC® C016779

Nikki's spending a week at North Hampton Hills as part of the school transfer program. The **GOOD NEWS** is that NHH's super-cool and preppy. The **BAD NEWS?** Nikki's nemesis MacKenzie started there two weeks ago!

Can Nikki and MacKenzie

overcome their differences

and become BFFs . . .

Best FRENEMIES FOREVER?!

NOOOOOO ☹!!

I CAN'T believe this is actually happening to me!!

I just found out yesterday that I'm going to be attending North Hampton Hills International Academy for one week as part of a student exchange program!

Yes, I know. It's a VERY prestigious school, known for its outstanding students, rigorous academics, chic uniforms, and beautiful campus that's a twist between Hogwarts and a five-star luxury hotel!

Most students would give up their CELL PHONES for a chance to attend there.

So WHY am I totally FREAKING OUT?!!

Because it's ALSO the school that a certain DRAMA QUEEN just transferred to ☹!

Yes, it's true! Unfortunately . . .

MACKENZIE HOLLISTER ATTENDS
NORTH HAMPTON HILLS!

2

Calling her a mean girl is an understatement. She's a RATTLESNAKE in lip gloss and hoop earrings and blond hair extensions. . . .

I have no idea why she HATES my GUTS!

But you'll NEVER believe THIS!

According to the latest gossip (from her little sister, Amanda, to my little sister, Brianna), a few of the North Hampton Hills girls have actually been HATING on MacKenzie! . . .

THEY MADE FUN OF MACKENZIE
BECAUSE OF THAT VIDEO
WITH THE BUG IN HER HAIR!

AND WENT OUT OF THEIR WAY
TO MAKE HER LIFE MISERABLE!

But all of this gets even STRANGER!

I saw MacKenzie a few days ago at the CupCakery,
and she was hanging out with some of her new
friends. PRETENDING to be . . . ME!

It was so BIZARRE, I almost flipped out! I wanted to rush down to the local POLICE STATION and scream . . .

Thanks to MacKenzie, my life is a never-ending

DRAMAFEST!!

In just the past month or so, she has:

1. slammed me in the face with a dodgeball

2. stolen my diary

3. hacked into my newspaper advice column

4. accused me of cyberbullying her

AND

5. pretended to be ME.

Like, WHO does that?!!

Only a complete and utter . . .

SICKO!

After MacKenzie transferred, I was hoping I'd NEVER have to see her face again.

But NOOOO!!!

Next week I'll be stuck attending North Hampton Hills with a spiteful, lip-gloss-addicted IDENTITY THIEF ☹!

PLEASE, PLEASE, PLEASE let my BFFs, Chloe and Zoey, get assigned to that school too.

With them by my side, I can get through just about ANYTHING!

Including a PAINFULLY long, MISERABLE week with my WORST enemy!

☹!

I just got to school a few minutes ago, and the eighth-grade students are already buzzing about Student Exchange Week.

I'm dying to talk to Chloe and Zoey about it.

But right now I'm so SLEEPY I can barely keep my eyes open.

Yesterday my parents surprised me with a . . .

NEW PUPPY!

Yes, it's true! The Maxwell family has a dog!

Her name is Daisy, and she's a golden retriever.

She's a sweet, happy, wiggly bundle of energy.

I LOVE her SO much that I'm thinking about making a new designer fragrance for teens called . . .

PUPPY BREATH!!

Daisy is absolutely PERFECT ☺!! She's SUPERplayful and so silly that she makes me laugh.

Anyway, I was so stressed out about having to attend North Hampton Hills that I barely got any sleep last night.

Although Daisy didn't help matters. As much as I adore her, I'm starting to wish she had an ON/OFF switch, because . . .

THAT DOG NEVER SLEEPS!

And every time I drifted off to sleep, she'd get bored and lonely and want to PLAY. . . .

DAISY DECIDES TO WAKE ME UP!

By SCARING the SNOT out of me!

ME, BEING ATTACKED BY A FEROCIOUS
FURBALL IN THE MIDDLE OF THE NIGHT!

She was so cute that I couldn't stay mad. . . .

ME, SNUGGLING WITH DAISY
(AND TRYING TO GET HER TO SLEEP!)

OMG! I probably got LESS than seventeen minutes of sleep the ENTIRE night!

It's Daisy's fault that I'm tired and grumpy and will be SLEEPWALKING from class to class.

I'm almost too exhausted to even WORRY about Student Exchange Week.

I wish it were a REAL foreign exchange student program for some faraway, exotic place, like maybe . . . Paris, France!

I'd LOVE, LOVE, LOVE to spend a week in PARIS ☺! It's SUCH a romantic city!

I just turned in a project for French class about the Louvre art museum, which contains some of the world's most famous masterpieces.

I hope I get a decent grade on it since my report and hand-drawn illustrations took me FOREVER to complete!

Anyway, I just had the most brilliant idea!

Since I'm a library shelving assistant, I can use that as an EXCUSE to get out of the program.

I'll simply ~~ask~~ BEG our librarian, Mrs. Peach, to let me ~~hang out~~ HELP OUT in the library during Student Exchange Week.

School will be out for the summer soon, and there's a ton of work that needs to be done to get the library ready for next year.

So I am pretty sure she'll say yes.

PROBLEM SOLVED! RIGHT ☺?!

WRONG ☹!!

That's when Principal Winston made an announcement over the PA system about Student Exchange Week. He explained that the final week of the program would start on Monday, May 12, and those of us eighth-graders who hadn't already participated in a previous week would be receiving a letter with details about our host school assignment later today.

He reminded us that instead of being graded on class assignments, students will receive one credit for successfully completing the program. Any student failing to do so will end up one credit short for completing eighth grade and NOT be promoted to ninth grade!

As if all of that news wasn't BAD enough, he said the credit would have to be made up by attending SUMMER SCHOOL!

SORRY!! But as much as I HATE the thought of spending a week with MacKenzie, I HATE the thought of spending the ENTIRE summer in school EVEN MORE ☹!

This student exchange program was quickly turning into a MASSIVE HEADACHE!

Even though I felt overwhelmed, I decided to handle my problem in a very calm and mature manner.

So I went straight to the girls' bathroom. . . .

And had a COMPLETE MELTDOWN!!

☹!!

We just received our letters. . . .

FROM THE OFFICE OF
PRINCIPAL WINSTON

TO: Nikki Maxwell

FROM: Principal Winston

RE: EIGHTH-GRADE STUDENT EXCHANGE WEEK

Dear Nikki,

Each year, all eighth-grade students at Westchester Country Day
Middle School participate in Student Exchange Week with local
schools. We feel this helps to foster community and good citizenship
between students and faculty at the host schools. Participation is
mandatory for YOU to meet your eighth-grade requirements.

Next week you will be attending NORTH HAMPTON HILLS
INTERNATIONAL ACADEMY (NHH). You are expected to be
on your best behavior and follow the NHH handbook. Photos for
student IDs will be taken on Friday, May 9.

If you have any questions or concerns, please feel free to contact me.

Sincerely,

PRINCIPAL WINSTON

19

Everyone was excitedly reading their letters and discussing their school assignments.

Principal Winston had also placed the master list right outside the office door.

I was at my locker writing in my diary when Chloe and Zoey rushed up to me, happily waving their letters in the air.

"OMG, Nikki! Guess what?! WE have the SAME school!" Chloe shrieked hysterically.

"WHAT?! NO WAY!" I blinked in surprise. "WE DO?! Are you sure?!"

I assumed that Chloe and Zoey had already checked the office list for my assignment.

"Chloe's right!" Zoey smiled. "WE'RE assigned to the same school! Can you believe it?!"

That news was almost too good to be true. I smiled and breathed a sigh of relief.

I had wasted all that energy worrying for no reason.

I was FINALLY starting to feel excited about the exchange program. It might actually be FUN!

"We're going to have a BLAST!" Chloe squealed. "Group hug, everyone!"

We were doing a group hug when Brandon walked up.

"Let me guess. The three of you have been assigned to the same school! Right?!" He smiled.

"YEP! So, what school did YOU get?" Zoey asked.

When Brandon held up his letter, Chloe and Zoey both screeched, "OMG!! BRANDON HAS THE SAME SCHOOL AS US!"

"This is KA-RAY-ZEE!" I giggled happily. "It seems almost UNBELIEVABLE that the FOUR of us have been assigned to—"

ME, FEELING TOTALLY CONFUSED!

"WHAT?!" I gasped in shock. "Wait a minute, guys! Are you sure?!"

But Chloe, Zoey, and Brandon didn't seem to hear me. The three of them were laughing and talking about how GREAT it was going to be to hang out with Brandon's best friend, Max Crumbly, at South Ridge Middle School.

Suddenly my stomach started to churn and I could taste the breakfast burrito I had eaten this morning. I bit my lip and tried to swallow the lump in my throat.

No one seemed to notice that I was upset. It was like I was invisible or something. And these people were SUPPOSED to be my FRIENDS?!

I didn't have any choice but to ask myself a very difficult question. . . .

WHY DID I FEEL LIKE A . . . GIANT BUCKET OF . . .

PUKE?!!! . . .

Suddenly everyone stopped talking and stared at me. "Nikki, are you okay?!"

That's when I closed my eyes and wailed. . . .

"MACKENZIE'S SCHOOL?!" they gasped.

I totally lost it right there in front of my locker as my three friends watched helplessly.

"That's TERRIBLE!" Chloe groaned.

"You POOR thing!" Zoey moaned.

"What CRUDDY luck!" Brandon muttered.

OMG!

I was so frustrated and angry, I wanted to . . .

SCREAM!!

There's just NO WAY I'm attending school with MacKenzie only to be publicly humiliated by her.

AGAIN!!

I guess this means I'll be signing up for summer school.

Sorry, Principal Winston!

But now that I know none of my friends will be at NHH with me, I'd rather poke my eye out with a dirty stick than be in your STUPID program!

☹!!

MONDAY—1:45 P.M.
IN BIOLOGY CLASS

Brandon and I are lab partners in bio and sit next to each other. I guess he must be worried about me or something, because he's been texting me nonstop. . . .

BRANDON: R U OK?

NIKKI: I'm fine. Just a little bummed out about the NHH fiasco.

BRANDON: How about I talk 2 Principal Winston about us switching schools?

NIKKI: ???

BRANDON: U go to South Ridge with BFFs. I go 2 Hogwarts. Then will U smile again?

NIKKI: R U kidding me? U would do that?!

BRANDON: Sure! 4 a friend.

We stared at our text messages and blushed. Then we stared at each other and blushed. All of this staring and blushing went on, like, FOREVER! . . .

BRANDON AND ME, TEXTING IN BIO

BRANDON: This class is so boring.

NIKKI: Totally agree. I'm trying to stay awake.

BRANDON: If I doze off, please SLAP me.

NIKKI: OK. LOL! Stop making me laugh or we'll both get detentions for texting in class.

BRANDON: Hey, at least U R smiling again!

By the time bio was over, Brandon had cheered me up. I was starting to feel like maybe it WASN'T the end of the world after all.

It was really sweet of him to offer to trade places with me and attend NHH. But MacKenzie has an even bigger CRUSH on Brandon than I do! She would happily give up lip gloss for the rest of her life to spend an entire week hanging out with him at NHH.

Sorry, girlfriend! But that is so NOT happening!

☺!!

MONDAY—7:00 P.M.
AT HOME

I was SO relieved when the school day was finally OVER!

It seemed to drag on FOREVER!

I really can't blame Chloe, Zoey, and Brandon for being excited about the student exchange program.

Hey, I'd be excited about it too if I were attending South Ridge Middle School.

The last thing I want is for my friends to ~~know~~ think I'm having a huge PITY PARTY just because I'm stuck attending North Hampton Hills with MacKenzie.

Anyway, when I finally got home from school, my bratty little sister, Brianna, was in the kitchen working on a Scouting project.

It seems like she's been trying to earn a cooking

badge, like, FOREVER. But, unfortunately, everything she makes turns out just AWFUL! . . .

BRIANNA, COOKING UP A REALLY HUGE MESS!

My curiosity finally got the best of me.

"Hi, Brianna! So, what are you making this time?" I asked.

"I've FINALLY perfected my chocolate pudding recipe!" Brianna exclaimed happily. "Now I just need to bake it for one hour."

"Actually, I don't think it's necessary to BAKE chocolate pudding. You should put it in the FRIDGE for one hour," I suggested.

"I'M the chef, and it's MY recipe! I say it goes in the OVEN for one hour! So THERE!" she said, and stuck her tongue out at me.

I just rolled my eyes at that girl.

But what did I expect from a spoiled wannabe chef who secretly uses boogers when she runs out of cupcake sprinkles?

Anyway, about forty minutes later I noticed a really foul odor. It kind of smelled like a garbage dump. On fire!

I rushed into the kitchen to check on Brianna.

"Nikki, take a look at my masterpiece!" She grinned as she held it out for me to see. . . .

"Doesn't this look DELISH?!!"

Brianna's "masterpiece" looked like a puddle of black tar with macaroni and several eyeballs stuck in it!

I actually threw up in my mouth! EWWW ☹!!

"I made this snack especially for my Scout meeting today. And if the girls like it, I'll finally earn my cooking badge!" she explained.

"Well, everyone loves, um . . . BURNT chocolate pudding, right?! YUM YUM!!" I stammered. "And it smells. Really strong. So, good luck with your badge."

"Thanks! I also added eggs for a crunchy texture," she said. "I learned that from the Chef's Choice TV show."

"You were supposed to CRACK the eggs first, NOT toss them in whole," I said.

"But the eggshells are the yummy crunchy part! Would you like to try some of my pudding? You're gonna LOVE it!" . . .

BRIANNA, TRYING TO SHOVE HER PUDDING
DOWN MY THROAT!

OMG! That's when I threw up inside my mouth
again ☹!!

Unless Brianna's cooking skills drastically improved,
I FEARED for the nutritional health of her future
husband and children. . . .

BRIANNA'S MENU FOR HER FAMILY

OMG! HOW were they going to SURVIVE on a
diet of BURNT chocolate pudding?!!

But I felt even SORRIER for those poor little girls who would be eating Brianna's pudding as a snack later.

Their frantic parents would be rushing them straight to the emergency room as soon as the Scout meeting was over.

WHY?

Because the entire troop would need to get their STOMACHS PUMPED due to Brianna's NASTY chocolate pudding.

The good news was that maybe she could have earned a stomach pump badge.

Anyway, when Brianna arrived back home from her Scout meeting, she was visibly upset.

"How did things go?" I asked.

"TERRIBLE! Everyone HATED my chocolate pudding!" she grumbled.

"Well, your pudding dish is empty. So even if the girls complained a little, they liked it enough to have eaten ALL of it!"

"No, they DIDN'T! After our troop leader contacted Poison Control, we were advised to dig a deep hole in the woods and bury the leftovers," Brianna ranted.

"Bury it in the woods?! But why?!" I asked.

"So no human or animal would accidentally EAT it. By the end of the meeting, we'd all earned our safety with toxic substances badge."

"Well, at least you and your troop earned a new badge. That's a GOOD thing, right?"

"WRONG! I was completely HUMILIATED!" Brianna sulked.

I didn't want to hurt Brianna's feelings, but it was true. Her pudding was better suited for filling potholes in the street than for human consumption.

"I'll NEVER earn a cooking badge!" Brianna sighed. "I'm the WORST cook EVER!!"

Brianna WAS the worst cook ever!

But she was also my little sister, and I didn't want to see her dream of earning a cooking badge destroyed.

I felt really bad for Brianna.

It seemed like only yesterday that I was six years old and totally obsessed with baking tiny burnt cupcakes in my very own Easy-Bake Oven.

I decided to talk to my parents about all of this.

But first I gave Brianna a big HUG!

Then I made her a huge bowl of her fave dessert— ice cream, ketchup, and raisins—to cheer her up.

BRIANNA EATS HER FAVE DESSERT
OF ICE CREAM, KETCHUP, AND RAISINS

It TOTALLY worked ☺!!

Within minutes she was smiling from ear to ear ☺!

But watching her actually EAT that stuff was
DISGUSTING! I just threw up in my mouth for the
THIRD time this evening.

EWWW!! ☹!!

TUESDAY, MAY 6—NOON
IN THE LIBRARY

I'm STILL totally stressed out about Student Exchange Week.

I dreaded attending North Hampton Hills because it meant dealing with MacKenzie and her crazy, mean-girl drama.

But if I DIDN'T participate, I'd be forced to make up the lost credit by attending summer school.

My situation was HOPELESS ☹!

Thank goodness Chloe, Zoey, and I had PE together during fourth period. I finally decided to talk to them about my problem.

Since the weather was nice, our class went outside on the soccer field to work on drills. The three of us took turns dribbling our balls around a set of plastic cones while discussing my latest life crisis. . . .

41

ME AND MY BFFS, DOING SOCCER DRILLS
AND DISCUSSING MY LATEST LIFE CRISIS

"Listen, Nikki, if you don't want to attend MacKenzie's school, maybe you should just explain your reason to Principal Winston," Zoey suggested. "I'm sure he'd understand."

"I totally agree," Chloe added. "If people knew even half of the AWFUL things that girl has done, no school would accept her as a student. Heck, her OWN parents would even REFUSE to HOMESCHOOL her!"

"I don't know, guys," I sighed. "MacKenzie stole my diary and kept it for twelve days! Remember? There was a lot of SUPERpersonal stuff in there that I wouldn't want ANYONE to know, especially Principal Winston."

"I think it's about time you stood up for yourself, Nikki!" Chloe argued. "You can't let MacKenzie continue to get away with the things she has been doing!"

After agonizing over my situation for what seemed like forever, I finally made up my mind. I knew exactly what I needed to do. . . .

44

"Thanks, guys! You're the best friends EVER! I know I need to do this. But just the thought of dealing with MacKenzie and her drama makes me SICK to my stomach!" I grumbled.

"Even if MacKenzie gets mad at you, what can she do?! TATTLE about some of the trivial stuff she read in your diary? Big fat hairy deal! At worst, you might get a few days of after-school detention," Chloe fumed.

Wait a minute!! A few days of DETENTION?!

"Yeah, it won't be the end of the world," Zoey agreed. "You'll get over it!"

Sorry, but it WILL be the end of MY world!! When my parents KILL ME ☹!

I could NOT believe my BFFs could be so insensitive.

"So . . . you both realize I didn't just write about the CRAZY stuff I did. I ALSO wrote about the CRAZY stuff WE did." I reminded them about . . .

45

Joyriding in the library . . .

Making prank calls on the school phone . . .

Sneaking into the boys' locker room . . .

Pretending to be on the football team . . .

Wandering the halls with a garbage can instead of a hall pass . . .

SQUEAK!!
SQUEAK!!

Smuggling eight dogs into the school . . .

← DOGS

BOOKS
FOR
LIBRARY

AND the fact that we've been SECRETLY
hanging out in the JANITOR'S CLOSET, like,
FOREVER. . . .

"That's not even everything we've done," I ranted. "Forget detention. WE'LL probably get a one-week SUSPENSION!"

Suddenly Chloe and Zoey got really quiet.

They both stared at me in total disbelief.

"Did you j—just say 'WE'?!" Zoey finally sputtered.

"Um, on second thought, reporting MacKenzie might NOT be the best way to handle things," Chloe muttered. "Did I mention that I'm ALLERGIC to suspensions?"

Okay, now I was starting to get a little ticked off.

I know Chloe and Zoey are supposed to be my BFFs. But it seemed like they thought ratting on MacKenzie was a really good idea until they realized that they might end up getting in TROUBLE along with me.

"So NOW you both think talking to Principal Winston might NOT be such a good idea after all? Then what am I supposed to do about Student Exchange Week?"

"Well, Nikki, you can always try to look on the bright side," Zoey offered.

"There ISN'T a bright side!" I grumped.

"Sure there is!" Zoey grinned. "You'll finally know what it's like to attend Hogwarts, but without the MAGIC classes!"

"Yeah, and their school uniforms are classy, chic, and SUPERcute!!" Chloe giggled.

I just rolled my eyes. Chloe and Zoey were no help WHATSOEVER!!

If I'm really lucky, maybe I'll find some NEW BFFs at North Hampton Hills!

☹!!

OMG! OMG! OMG!

I CANNOT believe what just happened to me in French class today (which, BTW, I had during seventh period due to standardized testing)!!

I'm so FREAKED OUT right now I can barely write this!

My heart is POUNDING, and it feels like my head is about to EXPLODE!

MUST. CALM. DOWN!!

It all started when my French teacher, Monsieur Dupont, returned my report about the Louvre, the world-famous art museum located in Paris.

It was seven typed pages and included several detailed illustrations that I'd personally drawn. I almost FAINTED when I saw my grade. . . .

ME, SHOCKED AND SURPRISED THAT
I GOT AN A+ ON MY REPORT!

I know, right?

But when my teacher asked me to stay after class because he wanted to talk to me about my report, I started to panic.

What if he thought I had cheated on it by plagiarizing or something ☹?!

I could understand why he might have been a little suspicious.

I'm definitely NOT the best student in his class, and I have to work really hard just to get a B.

But I actually ENJOYED writing my report!

I was SUPERinspired and motivated because the topic was art, and I really LOVE art!

Anyway, after class I went up to talk to my teacher.

I was really nervous and my stomach felt queasy.

But mostly I was praying I wouldn't THROW UP all over his desk! . . .

ME, TALKING TO MY TEACHER
ABOUT MY REPORT?!

Thank goodness THAT didn't happen!

Instead, I stood there clutching my report while my teacher raved about how impressed he was with my work. Then things got a little strange.

"Nikki, I think you'd be PERFECT for an honors French program this summer. You're such a talented artist, and the program's focus is art history and French culture. Would you be interested in participating?"

"Well, is it the ENTIRE summer?" I asked hesitantly. I did NOT want to attend summer school.

"I think it's about ten days in August. A group of students from area schools will be traveling to Paris to visit the Louvre and other historical landmarks!"

That's when I almost fainted.

AGAIN!!

"OMG! Did you just say a TRIP TO PARIS TO VISIT THE LOUVRE?!" I screeched excitedly. "YES! I'D LOVE TO GO TO PARIS!!"

"Great! The only slight complication is that the all-expenses-paid trip is being sponsored by the foreign languages department at North Hampton Hills International Academy. So I need to contact them to get all the details. But I'd be happy to recommend you for the program."

Guess what?! I almost fainted a THIRD time when he mentioned North Hampton Hills!

"Actually, Monsieur Dupont, I'm supposed to be attending North Hampton Hills next week as part of our Student Exchange Week!"

"PERFECT! Then I'll contact their foreign languages department and arrange for you to follow up with them while you're there visiting. I'll also forward a copy of your report and artwork. I'm sure they will be as impressed as I am."

"Thank you SO much for considering me!" I gushed. "It's such a wonderful opportunity!"

Then I calmly walked out of the classroom and gleefully did my Snoopy "happy dance" all the way back to my locker. . . .

ME, DOING MY SNOOPY "HAPPY DANCE"

SQUEEEEEEEE ☺!!

I can't believe I might actually be going to

PARIS, FRANCE!! . . .

. . . AS AN INTERNATIONAL EXCHANGE STUDENT!

So now I need to really impress the North Hampton Hills foreign languages department. They need to know that I'm smart, disciplined, dedicated, and an outstanding student.

Well, okay. Maybe I'm NOT all of those things!

But I AM interested in learning more about art history and French culture. And I'm nice, I'm friendly, and EVERYONE likes me.

Well, okay. Maybe not EVERYONE. And by "not everyone," I mean people like . . .

MACKENZIE HOLLISTER ☹!!

Anyway, I can't wait to tell Chloe and Zoey the wonderful news! They're going to FREAK!!

I thought my week at North Hampton Hills was going to be DOOM, GLOOM, and DREAD! But I was SO wrong!

It's going to be FANTASTIC!

WEDNESDAY, MAY 7—5:30 P.M.
AT HOME

Chloe and Zoey were SUPERhappy for me when I told them the unbelievable news about Monsieur Dupont and the possible trip to Paris. Yesterday we talked on the phone and then texted each other until almost midnight.

And today I received even MORE exciting news during lunch!

It was a delivery confirmation e-mail that my North Hampton Hills SCHOOL UNIFORM had just been delivered to my house.

SQUEEEEE ☺!!

I'll just be borrowing the uniform for one week and then returning it to the school. But STILL ☺! Chloe, Zoey, and I were so excited.

"I'll text you photos as soon as I try it on!" I told them as we ate lunch.

61

But they insisted on coming over to my house after school to hang out, and I agreed.

As soon as Chloe and Zoey saw the box, they immediately started SPAZZING OUT....

They were acting like I was opening a birthday present or something.

"Come on, guys!" I giggled. "CHILLAX! It's just a uniform."

But OMG! My new uniform was . . .

AWESOME!

I have to admit, when I first saw MacKenzie in her uniform, I was SUPERimpressed.

She looked SO smart and mature.

And nothing at all like the shallow, lip-gloss-addicted DRAMA QUEEN that she really is.

MacKenzie is going to be very shocked and surprised to see ME at HER school on Monday.

But I plan to ignore her and stay focused.

My major goal is to snag that trip to Paris!

And absolutely NOTHING—not even MacKenzie Hollister—is going to stand in my way!

I put on MY uniform and stood in front of the mirror with a huge smile plastered on my face.

I thought it looked really sharp on me.

And my BFFs totally agreed! . . .

CHLOE AND ZOEY, ADMIRING
MY CLASSY NHH SCHOOL UNIFORM

Then I got an unexpected SURPRISE!

My BFFs told me how proud they were of me and gave me a pink sparkly gift bag with the Eiffel Tower on it.

Inside was a box of Godiva chocolates, an English-to-French translation book of common phrases (like "Where is the bathroom?"), and the newest issue of *That's So Hot!* magazine.

"Nikki, this mag has great tips on being an international exchange student! It'll help you prepare for your trip!" Chloe explained.

I thanked my BFFs for the gifts and for always being there for me. Then I gave them both a big hug.

I'm already starting to miss them, and I haven't even left for North Hampton Hills yet.

Chloe and Zoey are the BEST. FRIENDS. EVER!! ☺!

I DREAD taking school photos! But tomorrow is picture day for everyone participating in Student Exchange Week.

We have to report to the WCD library during first period to take photos for our student IDs, which we are required to have for the program.

In geometry class my teacher was at the board figuring out a problem using the Pythagorean theorem.

But I was at my desk trying to figure out a much more complex problem. WHAT was I going to wear in my photo?

I pulled out my new *That's So Hot!* magazine and placed it on top of my math book. I was flipping through the fashion section for ideas when I spotted an ad. . . .

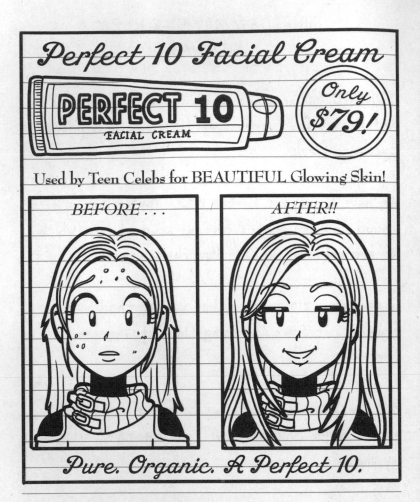

Hey, I wasn't STUPID!

Everyone knows the "before" and "after" photos in these types of ads are totally FAKE.

Which also means Perfect 10 facial cream is probably FAKE.

But the ad also said "Used by Teen Celebs for Beautiful Glowing Skin!"

And if it's good enough for THEM, then it's good enough for ME!

I was amazed to discover that not only is Perfect 10 pure and organic, but it's made from fancy ingredients like honey, plain Greek yogurt, blueberry extract, grape-seed oil, figs, seaweed, moon dust, and spring water.

OMG! I am DYING to try it!

Although I am fine with my dorky cuteness, I would much rather be mistaken for a glam teen celeb by people at North Hampton Hills ☺.

The only problem was that Perfect 10 is $79!

YIKES ☹!!

Sorry, but I was NOT about to let money stand in the way of achieving my dream!

I decided to create my very OWN Perfect 10 facial cream! But my cheap knockoff is going to be made from ingredients my mom already has in her kitchen. And instead of costing $79, it's basically FREE ☺!

Who knows, my very creative and ingenious idea might one day make me a BILLIONAIRE! . . .

THE DORKY GIRL'S HOMEMADE FACIAL CREAM FOR GORGEOUS GLOWING SKIN

WHAT YOU'RE NOT GOING TO NEED:

Are you basically BROKE, with a life savings of $3.58 secretly hidden in your sock drawer?

Is your mom adamantly REFUSING to give you $79 for Perfect 10 because she says she'd rather use the money to buy GROCERIES since your family can't EAT facial cream for dinner?

If you answered YES to either of these questions, then below is a list of the things you WON'T need.

I've already crossed out EVERYTHING on this list FOR you!

You're WELCOME ☺!!

~~Honey, Greek yogurt (plain), blueberry extract, grape-seed oil, figs, seaweed, moon dust, and natural spring water.~~

WHAT YOU'RE GOING TO NEED:

To keep things simple and save money, you'll be using ingredients you ALREADY have in your kitchen.

INGREDIENTS NEEDED
FOR THE DORKY GIRL'S
HOMEMADE FACIAL CREAM

Instead of honey, use pancake syrup.

Instead of plain Greek yogurt and blueberry extract, use Princess Sugar Plum Very Blueberry yogurt cups.

Instead of grape-seed oil, use grape juice.

Instead of figs, use fig snack cookie thingies.

Instead of seaweed, use canned spinach.

Instead of moon dust, use one package of Missy's hot cocoa mix.

Instead of spring water, use water from your kitchen faucet along with six ice cubes.

DORKY GIRL'S 10 STEPS TO BEAUTY

STEP 1: Sneak into the kitchen after your parents go to bed. Then they won't be all up in your business and asking you STUPID questions, like "Are you going to PAY for all the food you're wasting?"

STEP 2: Dump three blueberry yogurts into a large mixing bowl and put the empty containers back in the fridge so no one will suspect that YOU ~~stole~~ used them <evil grin>.

STEP 3: Stir in one cup of grape juice and a half cup of pancake syrup.

STEP 4: Eat the crust off six fig snack cookie thingies and add the fig stuffing to the mixture in the bowl.

STEP 5: Add in one teaspoon of cocoa mix and one tablespoon of canned spinach.

STEP 6: Stir the mixture for three minutes and then let it sit for ten minutes. Be aware that it may attract flies, and shoo them away.

STEP 7: Chillax and enjoy a cool, refreshing cup of ice water, because you've probably worked up a sweat and are pretty thirsty by now!

STEP 8: Smear the homemade facial cream all over

your face and let it dry. If there are any dead flies stuck to your face, remove them immediately for sanitary reasons.

STEP 9: Store leftovers in a covered container in the fridge for six additional facials. Or pour contents into a blender and blend on high for sixty seconds for a delicious Very Blueberry smoothie.

STEP 10: Go to bed and get plenty of beauty rest. When you wake up in the morning, remove your facial cream with warm water and a soft cloth.

You will be AWESTRUCK by the BEAUTIFUL, GLOWING, and RADIANT reflection in your mirror!

My miraculous homemade facial cream seems to be working, because my skin is tingling.

I ALREADY look and feel more beautiful ☺!! . . .

MY HOMEMADE FACIAL CREAM!

I can hardly wait to see the final results!

SQUEEEEEE ☺!!

Now it's time for ME to get some beauty rest.

When Brandon sees me tomorrow, he'll hopefully be so captivated by my magical, mystical, and miraculous BEAUTY that he'll profess his undying LOVE for me.

Or at least notice that my zits have cleared up!

☺!!

As soon as my alarm clock went off this morning, I hopped out of bed, giddy with excitement! I couldn't wait to see my beautiful, glowing, radiant skin.

I thought for sure I'd look like I belonged on the cover of *Teen Vogue* magazine.

I rushed into my bathroom, washed my face with warm water, and glanced in the mirror.

That's when I heard a very familiar voice screaming in horror!

Unfortunately, the voice was MINE.

I was screaming because my face was . . .

NEON BLUE!!

OMG! I looked like PAPA SMURF'S long-lost, half-human, very homely DAUGHTER. . . .

ME, IN THE MIRROR SCREAMING!!

I wanted GLOWING skin!

Not GLOW-IN-THE-DARK skin!

I was in complete shock and just kept shrieking,

"OMG! OMG! OMG! I'M BLUE! I'M BLUE!"

I guessed that it was from all those artificial colors in Brianna's Very Blueberry yogurt and the grape juice.

I tried scrubbing my face with soap, but the bright blue color would NOT come off!

My first thought was to give up and stay home.

I could spend the entire day just sitting on my bed, staring at the wall and SULKING ☹!

Which, for some reason, always makes me feel better ☺!

But that was not an option. I needed to take that student ID photo or I wouldn't be allowed to attend North Hampton Hills.

My chance to go to Paris would be RUINED ☹!!

I scrounged around in the hall closet until I found my dad's weird-looking SKI MASK that he wore while snowblowing during blizzards.

I didn't have a choice but to wear it to school to hide my blue face ☹!

I quickly got dressed and snuck into the kitchen, carefully avoiding my family members, and grabbed a cereal bar.

OMG! If Brianna saw me in that ski mask, my life was going to be in immediate DANGER!

Brianna would take one look at me, scream

"BURGLAR!"

and then violently attack me with a frying pan.

And until my bruises healed, I'd be black and blue!

And, um . . . BLUE!

How bizarre would THAT be?!

Anyway, when I arrived at school, every single student in the hall just stopped and stared.

Between my chic outfit and my dad's ski mask, I looked like a wannabe burglar with a wicked sense of fashion. I finally made it past all the gawkers to the janitor's closet and texted Chloe and Zoey. . . .

NIKKI: HELP!! EMERGENCY!! I'M IN THE JANITOR'S CLOSET!

Very soon Chloe and Zoey came rushing in. They took one look at me and FROZE with their mouths dangling open.

That's when Chloe grabbed a mildewy mop and brandished it at me menacingly. "WHO ARE YOU?

AND WHAT DID YOU DO WITH OUR FRIEND NIKKI?" she snarled.

"Listen, YOU! I have a dangerous weapon! And I'm NOT afraid to use it!" Zoey said, digging through her purse. "Wait! It's in here somewhere!"

Finally she pulled out her cell phone and pointed it right at me like it was loaded or something.

"DON'T MOVE!! Or I'll, um . . . SHOOT!!" she yelled.

I just rolled my eyes at my friends.

Apparently, Chloe was going to MOP me to death while Zoey recorded it on her cell phone.

Then WHAT were they going to do?!

Post it on YouTube?!

"Both of you! Just CALM down!" I said. "It's ME!"

"Sorry, but we don't know anyone named MIA!" Chloe said, narrowing her eyes at me. "Now, WHERE'S Nikki?!"

Okay, I'd had quite enough. I grabbed that mop from Chloe and resisted the urge to smack her with it.

"IT'S ME! NIKKI MAXWELL!"
I yelled.

Both Chloe and Zoey looked relieved. "NIKKI!"

Then Zoey gave me a puzzled frown. "If you don't mind me asking, WHY are you wearing a ski mask?"

I hesitated, trying to come up with a logical explanation.

But there was no intelligent way to say "I turned myself into a mutant blueberry because I wanted to look PRETTY."

So I decided to just stick with the facts. . . .

"WHAT?!!" Chloe and Zoey exclaimed. That's when I totally lost it!

"I'm BLUE!" I wailed. "You gotta help me!
I'm BLUE!!"

But my BFFs must have thought I had invited
them to the janitor's closet for a PITY PARTY
or something because I was feeling, um . . .
BLUE!

"Poor thing!" Chloe pouted. "Don't worry! We'll
cheer you up and put a smile back on your face!"

"Nikki is bery, bery SAD!" Zoey said in an annoying
baby voice. "I tink she needs a willy big hug!"

They both grabbed me and gave me a big bear hug.

"Now does Nikki feel better?" Zoey asked. "Because
we WUV you! We willy do!"

"You DON'T understand!" I said, snatching the ski
mask off my head. "SEE?!"

Chloe and Zoey just stared at me in shock for what
seemed like forever. Then they shrieked . . .

"Your FACE!" Zoey gasped. "It's like . . . cobalt blue! Sort of . . ."

"No, it's WAY worse." Chloe grimaced. "It's more like, um . . . toilet-bowl-cleaner blue! Or maybe . . ."

"SMURF BLUE!!" Chloe and Zoey said excitedly.

"Who CARES what shade of blue it is? I can't take my student ID photo like this!" I muttered, flushing red with embarrassment.

Which meant right then my face was probably a vibrant shade of purple.

Like, grape Popsicle purple!

I continued. "I can't get the color off! And now I have to wear a ski mask for the rest of my life! Do you know how HUMILIATING it will be to wear a ski mask to my WEDDING?" I ranted. "WELL, DO YOU?!"

"Nikki, just calm down!" Chloe said.

"I'm supposed to be getting my student ID photo for North Hampton Hills RIGHT NOW!

But I'm toilet-bowl blue and I look like an ALIEN CREATURE! And if I wear this stupid ski mask, I'll look like a BURGLAR. How am I supposed to go to Paris looking like THIS? TELL ME HOW!" I screamed.

"Girl, get a grip!" Zoey grabbed me by my shoulders to shake some sense into me. "Now explain how all of this happened."

"Yogurt," I muttered, blinking back tears.

"Wait a second! Did you just say 'YOGURT'?!" Chloe asked.

"Yes!" I sniffed. "I tried to make some fancy yogurt facial cream at home using Princess Sugar Plum blueberry yogurt and some other stuff. All I wanted was beautiful and radiant skin. But now I'm a blue . . . MONSTER!"

"Toilet-bowl-blue monster!" Zoey smirked. "But the good news is that it's just food dye, which is the same ingredient used in a lot of makeup.

Luckily, I have a mini pack of makeup remover wipes in my purse. So have a seat and watch me work my magic! Chloe, please assist. . . ."

CHLOE AND ZOEY CLEAN MY FACE!!

Within ten minutes my face was back to normal. Almost! Due to my homemade facial cream, my skin was now clear and silky smooth, with a radiant glow!

Chloe and Zoey were SO impressed, they begged to try some of my facial cream too.

Then we rushed down to the library and made it just in time to get our student ID photos. I think mine came out SUPERcute! . . .

NORTH HAMPTON HILLS
INTERNATIONAL ACADEMY

NIKKI MAXWELL
Student Exchange Week

Maybe my homemade facial cream will make me a BILLIONAIRE after all.

☺!!

Chloe and Zoey are the best friends EVER!

Thanks to them, not only did I look like a cover
model, but by lunchtime I had received a half
dozen compliments on my lip gloss, eye shadow,
and blush.

And I wasn't even wearing any!

As Chloe and Zoey dug into the huge mound
of chocolate pudding that was our lunch dessert,
I suddenly had a painfully nauseating flashback.

"EW! I'll NEVER, EVER eat that stuff again!!"
I muttered in disgust.

"Really, Nikki? So do you mind if I ask you a
question?" Chloe said.

"You want to know WHY I suddenly HATE

chocolate pudding, right?" I asked. "Well, it's kind of a long story. Brianna has been trying to earn a cooking badge. And earlier this week she made this AWFUL batch of pudding that looked like mud and—"

That's when Chloe interrupted me. "Actually, Nikki, I was going to ask you if I could EAT your chocolate pudding," she said as she reached over with her spoon and greedily gulped down the entire thing before I could answer.

"BUURRP! Oops! Excuse me!" Chloe giggled.

Did I ever mention that Chloe has the table manners of a barnyard animal?

Zoey folded her arms. "Now I'm REALLY curious. You stopped right in the middle, and I'm DYING to hear the rest of it."

"Okay, if you insist." Chloe grinned as she inhaled a deep breath. . . .

"Chloe, not YOU!" Zoey said, rolling her eyes. "I want to hear what happened with Brianna's cooking badge. Did she ever earn it?"

"No! Her burnt chocolate pudding was a DISASTER! And, unfortunately, she wants to try to cook ANOTHER snack for her NEXT meeting," I complained.

That's when Chloe and Zoey excitedly volunteered to come over to my house tomorrow to teach

Brianna how to make their specialty . . .

HAND-TOSSED PEPPERONI PIZZA!

I have to admit, Chloe and Zoey's pizzas are DELISH!!

Although I felt really bad for Brianna, I was more worried about a SECOND cooking disaster!

"Guys, I really appreciate you wanting to help my sister, but she can barely make a bowl of cereal. Pizza is going to be WAY too difficult for her!" I grumbled.

"Don't worry, Nikki," Zoey said. "Chloe and I will basically make the pizza FOR her!"

"That's right!" Chloe agreed. "The three of us will be right there supervising her. What could possibly go wrong?!"

EVERYTHING!!

☹!!

In spite of my BFFs' assurances, I still had a really bad feeling about Brianna the pizza chef.

Chloe and Zoey arrived this afternoon with the ingredients to make three pepperoni pizzas. One was for Chloe's family, one was for Zoey's family, and one was for Brianna.

Zoey's job was to make the dough, mine was to spread the tomato sauce on the dough, Chloe's was to place the pepperoni, and Brianna's was to sprinkle the mozzarella cheese on top. Everything was going fine until Brianna decided she wanted to do Zoey's job.

"Hey! I wanna throw that pizza dough up in the air just like Zoey!" Brianna squealed.

"No, Brianna!" I said, shooting her a dirty look.

Then she excitedly grabbed the dough. "Watch this! I'm gonna throw it really high!" . . .

BRIANNA TOSSES THE PIZZA DOUGH!!

"Brianna!" I yelled at her. "WHAT are you doing? Give that pizza dough back to Zoey right now, before you accidentally—"

BRIANNA MISSES THE PIZZA DOUGH!

OMG! I was so DISGUSTED!!

Brianna looked like the Pillsbury Doughboy's half-human little sister.

Our attempt to help her make a pizza had turned into a CATASTROPHE!

"Who turned out the LIGHTS?!" Brianna giggled.

Then she started staggering around the kitchen like a dough-covered ghost, yelling, "BOOO! BOOOO!" as if it were Halloween or something.

Chloe and Zoey couldn't help but crack up at my bratty little sister's CRAZY antics.

But this situation was NOT a joke!

Brianna had totally RUINED the snack she was preparing for her Scout meeting!

AGAIN!!

Chloe and Zoey each tried to give Brianna their pizza, but I wouldn't let them.

The pizzas they had made were supposed to be dinner for THEIR families.

"But HOW am I supposed to earn my cooking badge with no PIZZA?!" Brianna whined.

"Sorry, Brianna!" I said sternly. "But if you hadn't been GOOFING around, you would NOT be wearing your pizza dough right now! All of this is YOUR fault!"

So, unfortunately, Brianna didn't earn her cooking badge by making pizza.

But she definitely could have earned a new badge for . . .

☹!!

MONDAY, MAY 12—7:50 A.M.
IN THE NHH OFFICE

I barely slept last night, and by morning I was a nervous WRECK! I felt like a 105-pound bundle of jittery nerves in a chic North Hampton Hills school uniform.

I stood in front of my mirror, plastered a fake smile across my face, and practiced introducing myself to imaginary NHH students.

"Hi, I'm Nikki Maxwell, and I'm from Westchester Country Day Middle School!"

"Hi, I'm Nikki Maxwell, and I'm looking forward to my week here at North Hampton Hills!"

"Hi, I'm Nikki Maxwell, and right now I'm so gut-wrenchingly nervous, I need to find the nearest bathroom and THROW UP! Be right back!"

But when I set foot on the campus, I forgot my nervousness. I was totally blown away again by the pure AWESOMENESS of North Hampton Hills! . . .

OMG! It is the most FABULOUS school I've ever seen in my entire LIFE!

Manicured lawns and dozens of trees give it a peaceful, parklike atmosphere.

The interior of the school is even more impressive. The main entrance has a huge fountain that is even LARGER than the one at the mall. There are tall columns, arched hallways, shiny marble floors, elegant chandeliers, and a courtyard with a fishpond and a rose garden!

I feel like a traitor even thinking this, but NHH makes Westchester Country Day look like a basic, no-frills daycare center!

When I got to the office (which looks like the lobby of a luxury hotel), I filled out an exchange student registration form and handed my NHH student ID to the secretary.

"Good morning, and welcome to North Hampton Hills!" She smiled. "So, you're Nikki Maxwell? We have a new transfer student from your school. Do you know MacKenzie Hollister?"

"Um, actually, I do," I answered. "We had lockers right next to each other."

She glanced around the room to make sure no one was listening, leaned toward me, and then whispered, "Most of the kids here are wonderful. But there are a few you'll want to avoid. They can be a bit . . . snobbish."

"Thanks! But you don't have to worry," I assured her. "I've known MacKenzie for a long time, and I'm used to her drama. I'll be just fine."

The secretary blinked in surprise. "Actually, it's NOT MacKenzie I'm warning you about. She's such a nice, sweet girl! And friendly, too," she gushed, and turned back to her computer.

I just stared at that lady like she was crazy, because OBVIOUSLY we were NOT talking about the same person. Who would use the words "NICE," "SWEET," and "FRIENDLY" to describe MacKenzie Hollister, the most selfish, manipulative SHE-SNAKE in the world?!

It was quite apparent that this secretary was yet another of MacKenzie's many hapless victims. She had SLITHERED into this office and somehow BRAINWASHED this poor woman.

"Please have a seat, dear," the secretary said. "A student ambassador will be here any minute to give you a tour of the school. I hope you have a fun week!"

"Thank you," I said as I slowly backed away from her desk and sank into a large plush chair.

My nervous stomach was starting to make garbage disposal sounds again. I suddenly felt really queasy as a wave of despair rushed over me.

Maybe coming to North Hampton Hills was NOT such a good idea after all.

☹!!

MONDAY—11:10 A.M.
AT MY NHH LOCKER

I was still waiting in the school office when I spotted a gorgeous girl with auburn hair, a red designer purse, and matching stilettos.

She easily could've passed for MacKenzie's darker-haired twin sister.

Since she was holding a sign that said WELCOME, NIKKI!, I assumed she was my student ambassador guide for the week.

I grabbed my bag, thanked the secretary, and walked down the hall to meet her.

My heart pounded as I took a deep breath and introduced myself just like I had practiced in my mirror.

Yes, I know!

I could NOT believe that I actually said all of that EITHER. . . .

← ME

WELCOME,
NIKKI!

"Hi, I'm Nikki Maxwell, and I'm from Westchester Country Day Middle School. I'm looking forward to my week at North Hampton Hills. But right now I'm so gut-wrenchingly NERVOUS, I really need to find a bathroom and—!"

But I didn't get a chance to warn her I was about to THROW UP, because the girl dropped the welcome sign and practically TACKLED me! . . .

OMG! I'M SO HAPPY TO FINALLY MEET YOU, NIKKI! I'VE HEARD SO MUCH ABOUT YOU!

"My name is Tiffany Blaine Davenport, and I'll be your guide while you're here!" the girl squealed excitedly. "I have a feeling we're going to be BESTIES!"

"Um, it's nice to meet you, too, Tiffany!" I replied as I wondered exactly WHAT she had heard about me.

"Now that we've introduced ourselves, I think we should celebrate our new friendship." She giggled as she whipped out her cell phone. "IT'S SELFIE TIME!"

"Well, okay!" I said as I stood next to her and smiled for our picture.

Tiffany lowered her phone and looked at me like I was a huge zit that had just popped out on her FLAWLESS face.

"Um, SORRY! But there's no 'us' in the word 'SELF-IE'!" she quipped. "I'm so FIERCE that I need to take photos ALONE so there's enough space in the lens to capture ALL of MY exquisite beauty! Now, be a good BFF and get out of my way, PLEASE! By the way, I love your shoes!"

Then Tiffany gently shoved me aside in a really friendly manner.

How DARE that girl disrespect me like that! Especially after I'd only known her for, like, THREE minutes.

At least she was "nice" enough to let me participate in her supermodel-style selfie fashion shoot.

I got to stand off camera and vigorously fan her with my welcome sign to create the windblown hair effect.

Are we having fun yet?!

I couldn't help doing a giant eye roll.

While I stood there fanning Tiffany for what seemed like forever, I had a really BAD feeling (in addition to the intense cramping in my arms) that our so-called friendship was going to be a little unusual!

Tiffany wanted to be MY BFF ☺! But it appeared she wanted ME to be HER brainless zombie servant ☹!

Anyway, after we finally finished that awkward, spontaneous photo shoot, Tiffany helped me find my locker.

She introduced me to her BFFs, Hayley and Ava, who bragged nonstop about how the three of them were THE trendiest and most fashionable CCPs (Cute, Cool & Popular kids) at NHH, with a rep for throwing the wildest parties.

I couldn't help doing ANOTHER giant eye roll. Although they seemed to be SUPERimpressed with themselves, I wasn't at all.

Then Tiffany gave me a ninety-minute tour of the HUMONGOUS school. OMG! The place was so massive I could've ended up lost for days.

Once we finished the tour, we stopped by the office
to pick up my class schedule. . . .

NORTH HAMPTON HILLS Class Schedule		
NIKKI MAXWELL		
Class	Time	Teacher
History	8:00–8:50 a.m.	Mr. Schmidt
Geometry	9:00–9:50 a.m.	Mrs. Grier
Biology	10:00–10:50 a.m.	Mr. Winter
French	11:00–11:50 a.m.	Madame Danielle
Lunch	12:00–12:50 p.m.	N/A
Physical Ed	1:00–1:50 p.m.	Ms. Chandran
Study Hall	2:00–2:50 p.m.	Mr. Park

MY CLASS SCHEDULE

I really appreciated that Tiffany wanted to give me
some "invaluable advice along with the latest dirt" on all
of my teachers and classes. BUT it was definitely NOT
what I expected to hear from a student ambassador. . . .

TIFFANY'S ADVICE TO ME ABOUT MY NORTH HAMPTON HILLS CLASSES

HISTORY CLASS: "Mr. Schmidt is a senile old dude who loves ranting about when he attended NHH as a kid during the Stone Age. He's also blind as a bat and won't see a thing if you chill out in the back row and text your friends, polish your nails, or take a beauty nap. Not that I need a beauty nap. Although I think YOU could definitely use a few. No shade intended!"

GEOMETRY CLASS: "Mrs. Grier gives us pop quizzes once a week. But only a total loser would spend their weekends studying for them instead of hanging out and partying. I just copy answers from Hannah Stewart. She sits in front of me and always gets straight As. Just remember not to copy her NAME on your test. I did that once, and Mrs. Grier completely FLIPPED OUT and failed me! That lady is CRAZY!!"

BIOLOGY CLASS: "Mr. Winter's class is a breeze! Whenever he loses his lesson plan book (which happens a lot), instead of teaching he just shows us the same movie, *Jurassic Park*, which he says is a 'biting critique of the negative impact of unfettered cloning on modern civilization.' So far we've seen that movie eleven times. This MONTH! How does he keep losing his lesson plan book, you ask? It might have something to do with a SUPERsmart (and SUPERstylish) thief stealing it before class. You're welcome!"

PE CLASS: "This week we'll be going horseback riding on the trails. Get to the stable early to select your horse. Coco and Star are the friendliest and best behaved. WARNING! Avoid Buddy the Shetland pony. Despite his tiny size and cute name, he is NOT your buddy! That thing is a wild BEAST! Meet me at the stable ten minutes before class."

FRENCH CLASS: "Madame Danielle is the snobbiest and meanest teacher in the entire school. But right now she's also the most POPULAR because she's taking a group of students on an all-expenses-paid trip to Paris this summer. It's been like the Hunger Games around here, with kids fighting to the death for a spot. The most important thing to know about her is that she's secretly obsessed with sweets. If you want to get on her good side, just bribe her with a box of chocolate truffles. That's, like, the ONLY reason I'm not failing her class!"

Thanks to Tiffany, I found out that Madame Danielle is the head of the foreign languages department and the advisor for the trip to Paris.

I excitedly explained to Tiffany that my French teacher at WCD had recommended me for that program and that I was DYING to go to Paris!

I immediately rushed down to the office to request an appointment with Madame Danielle.

So now I'm scheduled to meet with her on Friday. SQUEEEEE ☺!!

Although, to be honest, she seems kind of mean. What if she HATES me?! Seriously, I'm already SCARED of her and I haven't even met her yet.

I'm just PRAYING she'll select ME to go to Paris.

It will be the BEST thing that has EVER happened to me in my ENTIRE life! . . .

At lunchtime Tiffany invited me to sit at a table with her and seven of her closest friends.

The NHH cafeteria is set up like the food court at the mall, but bigger and with better-tasting gourmet choices.

Although I was trying my best to be friendly, Tiffany was starting to get on my LAST nerve. This girl was so VAIN that she took a selfie, like, every ten minutes.

Next she asked me to go get HER a lunch since I was getting MY lunch. Then she asked me to dump HER lunch tray since I was dumping MY tray. And finally she asked me to carry HER books since I was carrying MY books.

OMG!

I totally LOST IT!

I yelled at her in front of the ENTIRE cafeteria. . . .

LISTEN, TIFFANY! I HAVE TO GO TO THE BATHROOM! SO WHILE I'M THERE, WOULD YOU LIKE ME TO PEE AND POOP FOR YOU TOO?!

ME, SCREAMING AT TIFFANY!!

But I just said that inside my head, so no one else heard it but me!

My first day here at North Hampton Hills has been very, um . . . EXHAUSTING!!

But unless I want to drop out of the student exchange program and give up all hope of going to Paris, I don't have any choice but to try to put up with Tiffany and her phony friends.

Hey, it's only for FOUR more days!

The GOOD NEWS is that things CAN'T get any WORSE!!

The BAD NEWS is that I might be really WRONG about the GOOD NEWS!

☹!!

Why does attending North Hampton Hills feel like I'm living in some INSANELY FREAKY alternate universe?

This morning Tiffany, Hayley, and Ava met me at the front door. Tiffany greeted me with a big hug and air kisses. "So, how is my new BFF today? Love your shoes!"

Hayley and Ava just looked me up and down with contempt and didn't say a word.

Jealous much?!

As we walked down the hall, Tiffany was so busy texting her latest selfie that she accidentally slammed into a guy carrying a book bag, a small box, and what looked like a plastic lightsaber.

Stunned, he lay sprawled on the floor next to his glasses. . . .

TIFFANY ACCIDENTALLY BUMPS INTO
A STUDENT AND KNOCKS HIM OVER!

"You clumsy IDIOT!" Tiffany snarled. "How am I supposed to send a text with you body-slamming me like this is the Super Bowl?"

"I'm s-sorry, Tiffany!" the guy stammered, slightly dazed as he slowly picked himself up.

"You science club geeks are so PATHETIC!" Hayley scowled. "And aren't you a little old to be bringing your toys to school?"

"I bet it's for show-'n'-tell! Well, you better get going, because the second-grade classrooms are in the elementary school building down the road." Ava laughed as the guy hobbled away, humiliated. "Get a LIFE!"

Tiffany resumed texting, and said, "I can't wait for you guys to see the two selfies I took this morning of me brushing my teeth and eating my pancakes! You're going to LOVE them!"

I stood there in shock, pondering whether these girls were extremely CRUEL or just mind-numbingly CLUELESS!!

I finally decided they were BOTH! And it made me so ANGRY I wanted to . . . SPIT!!

"Actually, Tiffany, it looked to me like YOU bumped into that guy," I said, highly annoyed. "Thank goodness he wasn't hurt."

She suddenly stopped texting and stared at me. Hayley and Ava folded their arms and wrinkled their noses like I'd just sprayed myself with a new fragrance called Fresh Cat Pee.

"Nikki! What's YOUR problem? I think you're just JEALOUS of my FAB selfies," Tiffany said accusingly as Hayley and Ava nodded in agreement.

"I don't have a problem. But if you text in a crowded hallway, you're probably going to bump into people," I tried to explain patiently.

All three girls gave me such giant eye rolls, I thought their eyeballs were going to pop out and roll down the hall. . . .

ME

TIFFANY AND HER BFFS,
EYEBALLING ME ALL EVIL-LIKE

"So, you're going to PRETEND to be Miss Perfect!"
Tiffany smirked. "Sorry, Nikki! But everyone here
has heard about YOUR reputation!"

"I know I'm not perfect," I said, defending myself.
"But I don't go out of my way to be unusually
CRUEL to people either."

"Oh, really? Then why did that MacKenzie Hollister girl transfer to this school to get away from YOU?" Hayley asked.

"According to the latest gossip, you made her life totally MISERABLE!" Ava said.

"That's NOT true!" I exclaimed.

"Well, I'D be MISERABLE too if someone RUINED my big birthday bash by sabotaging the chocolate fountain so that my BFF and I ended up completely drenched in chocolate!" Tiffany sneered.

"Yeah, and you CHEATED in your school's ART show, you CHEATED in the TALENT show, and you CHEATED in the charity ICE show!" Hayley taunted.

"Not to mention the fact that you SHOVED that poor girl into a Dumpster during the Sweetheart Dance! And PUSHED her down a SKI SLOPE! She could have been KILLED!" Ava said scornfully.

"Sorry, but NONE of those things are true!" I shot back. "They're all just nasty rumors that someone is spreading about me. I would NEVER, EVER do ANY of those HORRIBLE things!"

"Okay! So you DIDN'T toilet-paper MacKenzie's house in the middle of the night with some of your CCP friends?!" Tiffany asked, narrowing her eyes at me.

Hayley and Ava stared at me too, with complete disdain.

Of course all this made me REALLY mad.

"NO. I. DIDN'T!!" I screamed.

Then an awful memory suddenly popped into my head and kind of freaked me out.

You know, the memory from five months ago of me having a sleepover at Zoey's and toilet-papering MacKenzie's house in the middle of the night on New Year's Eve!! . . .

ZOEY

CHLOE

ME

ME AND MY BFFS TOILET-PAPER MACKENZIE'S HOUSE

"Well, um . . . OKAY!" I muttered. "Now that I think about it, maybe I DID pull a prank on MacKenzie by toilet-papering her house. But I didn't do ANY of the other scandalous stuff! So don't even go there!"

"Just admit it, Nikki! You're a Queen Bee just like ME! You ruthlessly go after whatever you want and will totally annihilate anyone or anything that gets in your way. I actually ADMIRED that about you! Until you turned on me like a pack of wolves," Tiffany growled.

"This is INSANE! I just suggested that you NOT text in a crowded hallway! How is THAT turning on you?" I responded.

"Sorry, Nikki! But I UNFRIEND YOU! Come on, girls, let's go!" Tiffany exclaimed. "I need to capture this very intense moment in my life with another SELFIE!"

Then Tiffany, Hayley, and Ava sashayed down the hall. I just HATE it when snobby mean girls sashay!

I went straight to the luxurious east wing, to my oversize locker, near a beautiful, SUPERexpensive chandelier, and started writing about everything that had just happened. . . .

ME, WRITING IN MY DIARY

Even though I was in a HUGE school filled with
hundreds of students, I suddenly felt all alone!

I swallowed the large lump in my throat as my eyes filled with tears ☹!

I NEVER thought I'd EVER miss my friends and my school, WCD, so much!

There was no doubt in my mind that Tiffany, Hayley, and Ava were definitely the mean girls that the office secretary had warned me about.

And the less I had to do with them, the better.

☹!!

TUESDAY—2:10 P.M.
IN STUDY HALL

My first four classes seemed to drag on FOREVER!

It didn't help that Tiffany was whispering about me and shooting me dirty looks.

It was like she hated me worse than knockoff designer purses.

Finally it was lunchtime. I grabbed a steak burger with waffle fries for lunch and yummy frozen yogurt with fresh strawberries for dessert.

Most of the kids in the cafeteria were sitting with their friends.

But since I didn't have any, I found an empty table in the very back near the garbage cans so I wouldn't bother anyone.

Then the strangest thing happened!! . . .

ME, SURPRISED THAT SOME GUYS
ASKED TO SIT AT MY TABLE

"I'm Patrick. And this is Lee, Drake, and Mario," he
said as they all took a seat.

"Hi, guys!" I smiled. "So, how did you know MY name?"

"EVERYONE knows your name!" Lee answered. "We've been hearing stuff about you for the past month! I guess you're famous at NHH!"

I took a bite of my hamburger and shrugged. "I almost hate to ask, but famous for WHAT?"

They looked at each other and then back at me. "Well, for your, um . . . reputation," Drake replied.

"That sounds more like INFAMOUS to me! If it's any of the rumors I heard this morning, NONE of them are true," I grumbled.

"THEY'RE NOT?!" the guys exclaimed, obviously disappointed.

"Actually, we were hoping they were," said Lee.

"Tiffany is on a power trip, and she runs this school like a prison warden. But we've heard she's really intimidated by you. We should form an alliance!" Mario said.

134

"An alliance? What kind of alliance?" I asked.

"Well, if you can help us, maybe we can help you!" Drake answered.

"Help you with what?" I asked, a bit suspicious.

"We're members of the science club. But to keep our funding we have to maintain a membership of at least six students in addition to our four-member executive board. Since we have less than that, we'll be losing our funding on Monday and won't be a club anymore," Patrick explained.
"And now Tiffany has convinced our student council president to replace us with her new selfie photography club. She said it would better serve the school since twelve people have already signed up."

"Well, have you ever tried a membership drive?" I asked.

"Yes, we had one in April. It was very successful and actually doubled our membership!" Lee said.

135

"That's great news! So how many members do you have NOW?" I asked.

"We went from TWO to FOUR members! But we still need six more. We put a sign-up sheet in the boys' locker room," Drake bragged. "Do you have any idea how many guys pass through there? Like, hundreds!"

"Come on! WHAT ABOUT GIRLS?!!" I shrieked. "No wonder no GIRLS signed up."

"I guess we messed up really bad. So will you help us?" Patrick pleaded.

"PLEEEEEASE!!!" the four of them begged.

"I'm really sorry, guys! But I don't think there's really anything I can do. Have you thought about joining the selfie club? It might be fun." I shrugged.

"Well, why don't we consider taking more, um . . . DRASTIC measures?" Patrick suggested.

"What do you mean by 'drastic'?" I asked.

The only DRASTIC measure I wanted to take was to stage an intervention for Tiffany to cure her annoying SELFIE ADDICTION. . . .

TIFFANY GETS MEDICAL TREATMENT FOR HER SELFIE ADDICTION!

"Drastic, like . . . I don't know," Drake said. "Maybe you could steal her diary and blackmail her into dumping the selfie club?"

"You could slam her in the face with a dodgeball so hard she gets amnesia and forgets all about her new club?" Lee suggested.

"You could put a bug in her hair and post it on YouTube so she'll transfer to a new school out of sheer humiliation?" Mario suggested.

I was getting sick and tired of people repeating all those rumors. "I KNOW!" I yelled sarcastically. "WHY DON'T I JUST PUSH TIFFANY OFF A SKI SLOPE SO SHE'LL BREAK HER NOSE AND NEVER WANT TO TAKE ANOTHER SELFIE AGAIN?!"

The guys started cheering and high-fiving each other.

"PERFECT!!" Patrick shouted.

"BRILLIANT!!" Lee roared.

"AWESOME!!" Drake cheered.

"EXCELLENT!!" Mario yelled.

"Sorry, dudes! I was kidding! That was just SARCASM!" I grumbled.

"Well, can you at least come to our meeting after school on Friday?" Patrick pleaded.

"I don't think so. But what usually happens at these meetings?" I asked out of curiosity.

"Well, we start by suggesting a daily activity. Then we vote YES or NO and drop them in the ballot box. Then we open it and count the votes," Mario explained.

"So your club does cool stuff like conduct experiments, visit technology museums, and enter science fairs, right?" I asked.

"No! We usually just do reenactments of our favorite lightsaber fight scenes from the Star Wars movies. It's really fun and exciting!" Lee exclaimed.

So THAT explained why Patrick was carrying that small box and lightsaber this morning.

"I don't know, guys!" I sighed. "Just let me think about it, okay? Maybe we can meet here tomorrow during lunch to discuss it some more."

So that was our plan.

The guys thanked me and headed off to class feeling hopeful.

But deep down I already knew there wasn't much I could do to help them save their science club.

☹!!

I felt really bad for Patrick and all the guys in the science club.

Hey, I knew from personal experience what it was like to face the WRATH of Tiffany. I only have to deal with her for the rest of the WEEK. But those poor guys are stuck with her for the rest of the YEAR!

Tiffany is just a mean girl whose hobby is RUINING other people's lives.

And speaking of mean girls. . . .

I had a really good hunch WHO was spreading all those NASTY rumors about ME.

I glanced at the clock on the wall and grabbed my book bag to rush off to class.

Then I turned around, stopped dead in my tracks, and found myself face-to-face with . . .

MACKENZIE HOLLISTER,
STARING AT ME IN SHOCK AND HORROR!

142

MacKenzie looked like she had just seen a ghost! Then she was all up in my face like, um . . . my homemade FACIAL CREAM!

I was so mad at her that I could have SLAPPED her into tomorrow!

But I would NEVER do anything like that because I am a very peaceful and nonviolent person.

I'm also very ALLERGIC to BEATDOWNS!

When I last saw MacKenzie at the CupCakery on April 30, she was there with her new friends from NHH. But it was quite OBVIOUS she was pretending to be ME. It was like she had stolen and assumed MY life but had kept her OWN name.

MACKENZIE'S LIST OF LIES
(HOW SHE STOLE MY LIFE!)

MacKenzie said SHE:

1. Had a band called Actually, I'm Not Really Sure Yet

2. Had a record deal with Trevor Chase

3. Was crowned Sweetheart Princess at her Valentine's dance with Brandon as her date

4. Had an advice column in our school newspaper called "Miss Know-It-All"

5. Was a regular volunteer at Fuzzy Friends Animal Rescue Shelter

6. Ran a book drive for the school library

7. Won a cash prize for charity in an ice-skating event

And as if all of THIS wasn't deranged enough, MacKenzie had ALSO started a dozen rumors saying that I had done all of the CRUEL stuff to HER that SHE had actually done to ME!

Anyway, I pointed MY finger right back in HER face and shouted . . .

ME, STARING AT MACKENZIE
IN SHOCK AND HORROR!

Things suddenly got really, really tense.

"I wouldn't WANT your PATHETIC life, Nikki! Now, WHAT are you doing at MY school?!"

"I'm in the student exchange program. But I DREADED coming to North Hampton Hills because of YOU! I'm only here because I want the FREE trip to PARIS sponsored by this school! My teacher at WCD said I had a good chance. But I'm probably wasting my time, because I've heard that the trip advisor, Madame Danielle, is really mean unless you BRIBE her with chocolate!" I yelled.

"Well, just mind your business while you're here! I'm not going to let you ruin my life. You have no idea what I had to go through to get into this school!"

"MacKenzie, you have it SO easy! Everything is handed to you on a silver platter!"

"You're WRONG! I shouldn't even be at this school. I freaked out on the entrance exam and scored so low that my parents had to donate a ton of money to get me admitted. So, Nikki, you have no clue!"

I glared at MacKenzie.

And MacKenzie glared at me.

That's when we suddenly heard someone snicker, "OMG! What a DRAMAFEST! I wish I had a bucket of popcorn!"

MacKenzie and I both turned around and gasped!

TIFFANY was standing right behind us, FILMING us with her CELL PHONE!

She stopped filming and flipped her hair.

Then she stepped right in front of us and struck a GLAM pose.

MacKenzie and I both stared at her in disbelief as she made a duck face and took a quick selfie. . . .

147

TIFFANY TAKES A SELFIE
WITH MACKENZIE AND ME!

"Sorry, girls! But both of you came from that
TRASHY school Westchester Country Day! You'll
NEVER be good enough for North Hampton Hills!
And my video is all the proof I need. So don't

think for one minute you're going to come here and take over MY spot as QUEEN BEE! It's so NOT happening!"

MacKenzie and I stared at each other. There was no question that we'd pretty much HATED each other from the first day we met.

Then we BOTH stared at Tiffany, a selfie-addicted diva intent on DESTROYING both of our lives. She was probably the ONLY person we both HATED more than EACH OTHER!!

Tiffany looked at the photo and giggled. "I think our selfie came out SUPERcute! I can't wait for you to see it. I'll text copies to you both, okay? You're going to LOVE it! See you later! Oh, BTW, I ADORE your shoes!"

I was completely FLABBERGASTED!

In just a few hours Tiffany had gone from being my new BFF to my NOT-SO-FRIENDLY FRENEMY!

Like, WHO does THAT?!

It suddenly became very clear to me.

There was just NO WAY that I was going to SURVIVE this program.

☹!!

Having to deal with MacKenzie is really BAD!

And having to deal with Tiffany is HORRIBLE!

But having to deal with BOTH MacKenzie and Tiffany at the same time is enough to make me . . .

SCREEEEEEEEAM ☹!!

I seriously considered telling my mom I needed to stay home from school the rest of the week because I was really SICK and TIRED!

SICK and TIRED of MacKenzie trying to STEAL my life.

SICK and TIRED of Tiffany trying to RUIN my life.

I'm not sure how much MORE of their DRAMA I can take!

And if I had a choice, I'd much rather have a
COMPLETE MELTDOWN in the privacy of my
bedroom than at North Hampton Hills in front of
hundreds of students.

There were two girls at the locker next to mine, and
I couldn't help but overhear their conversation.

"Anyway, Tiffany said we need to sign up for
the selfie club right away so it'll replace the
science club. Although, to be honest, I'd much
rather be in the science club than fanning the hair
of CCPs for their photos," grumbled a girl with
a ponytail.

"I totally agree! I didn't even know we HAD a science
club," said her friend.

I decided to introduce myself. "Hi, I'm Nikki Maxwell.
I'm from Westchester Country Day, and I'm visiting
here as an exchange student."

"Hi, I'm Sofia, and this is my BFF, Chase," said
the girl with the ponytail. "Wait a minute! Aren't

YOU the Nikki who tried to close down Fuzzy Friends Animal Rescue Shelter?"

"And WHY do you HATE puppies?!" demanded Chase. "They're SO ADORABLE!"

I was like, JUST GREAT ☹!!

"Um, that wasn't ME! It was some other girl named Nikki," I lied. "She sounds like an AWFUL person. Personally, I LOVE puppies!"

Sofia and Chase nodded in agreement.

I continued. "I was just wondering if you guys were interested in joining the science club. They're having a membership meeting on Friday and will be planning exciting activities for next year. We need your ideas. It'll be fun!"

"And girls in science, technology, engineering, arts, and math are SUPERCOOL!" said Sofia.

"Right! S.T.E.A.M. rocks!" added Chase.

"GREAT! JUST WRITE DOWN YOUR IDEAS
AND BRING THEM TO THE MEETING!"

"I'll be hanging out with a few science club members
at lunch if you'd like to join us," I said.

"Okay!" Sofia and Chase smiled.

There was still a lot to be done, but maybe our plan to save the science club just might work.

Tiffany will have a HISSY FIT once she finds out that her selfie club is in jeopardy.

But I am SO over Miss Queen Bee and her shady girl squad of Wanna Bees.

I have three important goals: (1) avoid Tiffany and MacKenzie like highly contagious diseases, (2) help Patrick save the science club, and (3) convince Madame Danielle to give me that trip to Paris!

Then I am OUTTA HERE!

☺!

When I got to biology, Mr. Winter had "lost"
his lesson plan book again, which meant we'd be
watching _Jurassic Park_.

Finally, it occurred to me why he showed that
movie over and over again during class.

It was to DISTRACT his students! He needed them
to shut up and leave him alone so he could search the
Internet for a NEW TEACHING JOB at another
SCHOOL!

The poor guy looked SUPERstressed.

I suddenly felt really sorry for him.

Tiffany was at her desk talking to her friends, and
when she saw me she did the strangest thing.

She walked up to my desk and gave me a HUG that
seemed to last FOREVER.

"Nikki, I want to apologize for what happened yesterday," she said sweetly. "Things just got out of control. I didn't mean any of what I said, and you were right all along. So are we cool?"

I was shocked!

A CCP had NEVER apologized to me before!

MacKenzie would rather be buried alive in a polyester party dress from Walmart with knockoff designer shoes than EVER apologize to anyone.

This was almost too good to be true.

Maybe Tiffany wasn't as evil as I'd made her out to be.

I decided to give her ONE more chance. But I still didn't completely TRUST her.

"Hey, it's no big deal. We're cool." I smiled.

"YAY!" she exclaimed. "I've got my bestie back!"

157

Then she returned to her desk and started giggling and whispering to her friends.

The teacher was about to turn off the lights and start the movie when Tiffany raised her hand.

"Mr. Winter, I just wanted to let you know that I saw someone SWIPE your lesson plan book."

I was really surprised to hear THAT news!

Especially since Tiffany had already confessed to me that SHE had been stealing his lesson plan book all year.

Mr. Winter scowled and raised an eyebrow. "Well, thank you, Miss Davenport! And who might this THIEF be?"

I was shocked and appalled by the totally SCANDALOUS thing Tiffany did next.

She stood up, pointed right at me, and said . . .

TIFFANY, ACCUSING ME OF
STEALING THE TEACHER'S BOOK

I just stared at her in disbelief! I already knew
Tiffany was a mean and snobby selfie addict. But I
DIDN'T know that she was ALSO a pathological liar!

"Mr. Winter, th—that's NOT true!" I stammered.
"I didn't take your lesson plan book! And it's NOT
in my book bag! I'll show you. . . ."

The entire class gawked at me as I frantically
dumped the contents of my bag on my desk.

"See, Mr. Winter? It's NOT here in my—"

I stopped midsentence and blinked in confusion.

A large brown leather book that I had never
seen before in my life was lying on top of my
textbooks.

I shot a dirty look at Tiffany. She must have slipped
the teacher's lesson plan book into my book bag
during her apology hug.

That selfie-addicted SNAKE just shrugged and
smiled at me all innocentlike.

Mr. Winter quickly strode across the room and
snatched his book off my desk. . . .

ME, TOTALLY FREAKING OUT ABOUT
MY TEACHER'S BOOK!

"Miss Maxwell, we have a zero-tolerance policy for THEFT," he said firmly. "Just so you know, I WILL be speaking to Principal Winston about your despicable behavior!"

"But, Mr. Winter, you don't understand! I would NEVER—!"

"Save your EXCUSES for when you get back to Westchester Country Day!" he said coldly.

I just sat there, numb, with my heart pounding in my chest like a bass drum.

I could hear Tiffany and her friends snickering behind me.

I was beyond HUMILIATED!

I wanted to dig a really deep hole right there in the classroom, CRAWL into it, and DIE!!

Although I was still a bit traumatized by Tiffany and all the drama in biology, I was looking forward to hanging out with the kids from the science club during lunch.

Sofia and Chase sat at our table and shared their list of creative ideas for the club.

They both fit right in and got along really well with the guys.

I suggested that the Friday meeting in the science lab be a membership drive and PARTY, complete with Queasy Cheesy pizza.

Everyone LOVED my idea!

We all agreed to place science club sign-up sheets all around the school and not just in the boys' locker room.

Lee and Mario volunteered to handle the pizza and soft drinks. Patrick and Sofia agreed to do decorations. Drake offered to be our deejay and suggested a science-themed playlist that included his favorite old-school song, "She Blinded Me with Science."

That's when Chase excitedly suggested that the party theme be "Blinded by Science!" and volunteered to make matching posters.

She also had a brilliant idea for cool party favors that we could get SUPERcheap from the dollar store.

I reminded everyone how important it was to invite friends and other students to our science club party! Well . . . um, science club meeting.

Our goal was to show that science could be fun and exciting as well as interesting.

Anyway, everyone was so fired up that we completely lost track of time.

By the time we finished planning our event, lunch
was over and we had less than a minute to scramble
to our next class.

I wasn't all that worried about being late until
I realized it was PE.

Yesterday we'd spent the entire class discussing the
basics of horseback riding and how to do it safely.

And today we were actually going to be RIDING.

That's when I suddenly remembered Tiffany's
WARNING about the importance of getting to the
horse stable ten minutes EARLY to select a horse.

JUST GREAT ☹! I took off running and prayed
that I'd get there before it was too late.

I quickly got dressed in my riding outfit and rushed
out to the stable to sign up for a horse.

But, unfortunately, only ONE was left. . . .

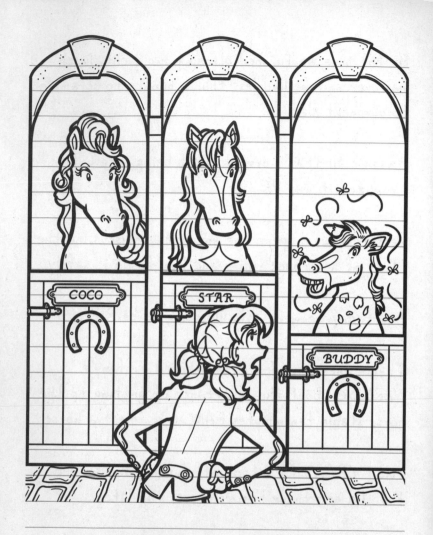

"BUDDY THE PONY?!"

I just stared at him in shock. He was the EVIL
horse . . . I mean, pony . . . that everyone was
afraid to ride.

"Look at that nasty, ugly BEAST!" Tiffany sneered from behind me. "I think poor little Buddy is absolutely TERRIFIED of you!"

I was so mad, STEAM was practically coming out of my ears. But there was also steam coming from another place . . . Buddy's backside! EWW ☹! OMG! The stench of his gas was AWFUL. That pony smelled like he'd eaten nineteen cans of baked beans and seven really dirty, stinky gym socks.

The entire class rode out of the stable to the trails, except for Buddy and me.

"Come on, Buddy! Let's go!" I groaned and tapped him with my feet.

Buddy gave me a dirty look and neighed loudly.

"Quit complaining!" I fumed.

He angrily stomped his foot and passed more gas. Then he dashed out of the stable and down the trail and turned into a wild bucking bronco. . . .

BUDDY TRIES TO KILL ME WHILE
I HOLD ON FOR DEAR LIFE!

Tiffany and Ava rudely pointed and laughed.

"Yee-haw! Ride 'em, cowgirl!" Ava yelled.

"Wow! This is the funniest rodeo CLOWN SHOW ever!" Tiffany giggled. "Nikki, you're a goofball!"

I could not believe those girls were making JOKES when I could have been seriously injured or even KILLED by that CRAZY horse. However, after ten minutes, Buddy must have exhausted all his negative energy, because he suddenly calmed down and trotted along the trail and back to the stable like a show horse.

Everyone, including my teacher, was impressed that I had tamed Buddy with my superior horsemanship skills. But Tiffany and Ava just glared at me and rolled their eyes.

When we got back to Buddy's stall, I fed him a carrot for his good behavior. Then he passed gas, smiled at me, grunted, and fell fast asleep.

My little pony was my best BUDDY ever! ☺!!

Chloe and Zoey stopped by after school today to see how things were going for me at NHH.

At first I tried to lie and tell them how wonderful everything was. But I finally broke down and told them the truth. It was a disaster!

MacKenzie was spreading nasty rumors about me and had pretty much stolen my life! Tiffany had secretly recorded me ranting about the French teacher, which meant I was NEVER going to be awarded that trip to Paris! And Mr. Winter thought I had stolen his lesson plan book and was going to report me to Principal Winston!

"Listen, Nikki, do NOT go back to that school!" Zoey pleaded with me. "Why are you punishing yourself like this?!"

"OMG! That place sounds HORRIBLE!" Chloe gasped. "How can you stand it?!"

170

That's when I burst into tears. . . .

WAAAAAAAH!!

"Listen, guys, you're right! But I've made new friends there, and I really want to say good-bye to them instead of just disappearing off the face of the earth," I said, sniffling.

So we all agreed that Thursday was going to be my last day at NHH, even if it meant having to attend summer school. Although I felt relieved this dramafest would be over soon, I couldn't help but feel a little worried about my friends in the science club. ☹!!

I was so stressed out about everything that I barely got any sleep last night.

My goal was to survive my last day at NHH. Things couldn't possibly get any worse, right?!

WRONG! During breakfast I got a text from MacKenzie!

She asked me to meet her at the fountain right before study hall to discuss OUR Tiffany problem. I texted "???," but she didn't respond.

During lunch the science club members sat at my table and chatted excitedly about the event tomorrow.

They thanked me for everything I'd done and told me the club had a special award they planned to give to me at the party. Then everyone started cheering.

I didn't have a choice but to break the bad news. "Actually, TODAY is going to be my last day at NHH. And even though I won't be able to attend the science club party, I'm sure it's going to be a huge success!"

I totally didn't expect what happened next.

"Nikki, if YOU'RE not going to be there, then why should we even bother?!" Patrick muttered in disappointment.

"I agree!" said Sofia. "You talked all of us into doing this, and now you're BAILING on us!"

"That's NOT fair!" everyone complained at once.

I had to tell them about the drama with MacKenzie, Tiffany, and Mr. Winter and how I needed to leave before things got even worse.

"But you told us to stand up to Tiffany and not let her close down our science club. If you leave early, YOU'RE letting Tiffany WIN!" Patrick argued.

I had to admit he had a good point. But when I explained that I was stressed out and leaving early might possibly resolve my problems, everyone finally understood.

I was really disappointed by what they did next.

"We're voting to cancel the science club meeting and allow it to become the selfie club," Patrick muttered. "Write 'YES' or 'NO' on your ballot and put it in the box, please. Nikki, you can count them."

I was like, JUST GREAT ☹!! As I counted the ballots I got a huge lump in my throat. There were six votes, and all of them were "YES!" for canceling the meeting.

My friends had given up and Tiffany had WON!

The rest of the day seemed to drag on forever.

I decided I'd clean out my locker and turn in my student ID card AFTER I met MacKenzie at the fountain. . . .

The first thing I wanted to know was WHY she had started all those nasty rumors about me. I was shocked when she told me her horror story. . . .

Tiffany and her friends had mercilessly teased
MacKenzie about that video with the bug in her
hair. So she started hiding out in the bathroom to
avoid them. . . .

Tiffany went out of her way to make MacKenzie's life absolutely miserable, and MacKenzie became a social outcast without a single friend. . . .

MacKenzie said she felt invisible because it seemed like all the students at NHH ignored her. So every day at lunch she sat all alone. . . .

Until one day she overheard some kids talking about the 15 Minutes of Fame talent TV show.

And when she mentioned that the famous producer, Trevor Chase, had come to WCD back in March and worked with her and the band Actually, I'm Not Really Sure Yet, the NHH students mistakenly assumed she was the leader of my band.

They were SUPERimpressed! And the more MacKenzie talked about MY life, the more attention she got, the more popular she became, and the more friends she made.

Until she got so carried away with her tangled web of lies that she'd all but assumed MY life!

And to keep NHH students from possibly finding out who I REALLY was, she'd started the nasty rumors about me to create even more confusion.

It was SURREAL!!

But suddenly MacKenzie and I were RUDELY interrupted!

By TIFFANY ☹!!

"Sorry, girls! But I need to take some selfies for my weekly fashion blog of the new makeup brand I'm wearing. The spot you're sitting in has the most flattering light in the entire school. SO GET LOST!" she exclaimed as she shoved us out of the way.

MacKenzie and I stood in front of the fountain, glaring at that girl. Tiffany stepped on top of our bench like it was a stage, took several photos of herself, and then frowned.

"Darn it! The sunlight is right over the fountain!" she complained as she climbed up on its ledge. "Now get out of my photo!"

"I have a better idea!" MacKenzie scoffed. "Why don't you go CHOKE on your cell phone!"

"Don't hate me because I'm beautiful!" Tiffany sneered as she teetered on the edge of the fountain in her heels, striking various poses.

MacKenzie and I exchanged glances. I think we both had the same wicked wish.

Suddenly Tiffany's foot slipped and she lost her balance. "WHOA!!" she gasped loudly.

MacKenzie and I just stared in disbelief as she wobbled back and forth and back and forth in slow motion, wildly flapping her arms like she was a baby bird trying to fly for the first time.

Just as Tiffany was about to topple into the fountain, she grabbed MacKenzie's right arm in an attempt to regain her balance. Which worked for only about two seconds. Because Tiffany then knocked MacKenzie off balance, and the two of them teetered over the edge of the fountain together.

That's when I vaulted onto the ledge and grabbed MacKenzie's left arm and pulled her in the opposite direction like she was the rope in a game of tug-of-war.

Now all THREE of us were teetering back and forth over the edge of the fountain like some kind of weird circus act, trying not to fall in.

It was only after I grabbed MacKenzie's waist and pulled with all my might that the three of us finally tumbled into a big heap on the marble floor next to the fountain. Hey, at least we weren't IN the fountain!

But somehow the force of us falling had launched Tiffany's cell phone into the air.

She watched in HORROR as it fell into the fountain with a big SPLASH and quickly sank to the bottom!

"OH NO! MY PHONE!! MY PHONE!!" she screamed hysterically. Then she DOVE right into the fountain after it!

Soon Tiffany's shrieks echoed through the halls of the school. "OMG! MY CELL PHONE IS RUINED! HOW AM I SUPPOSED TO TAKE A SELFIE WITHOUT MY PHONE?!!"

That's when I whispered to MacKenzie, "Since Tiffany's phone is all wet, I really think we should be nice and help her out!" . . .

MACKENZIE AND ME, TAKING VIDEOS OF
TIFFANY FOR HER FASHION BLOG ☺!!

Tiffany continued her rant. "MacKenzie and Nikki, I HATE both of you!! I know you did this to get even with me. For stealing Mr. Winter's lesson plan book and blaming Nikki! For pulling all those mean pranks on MacKenzie and making her life MISERABLE! And for trying to shut down that STUPID and WORTHLESS science club so we can have my FABULOUS new selfie club! It's all YOUR fault I RUINED my precious phone! I promise you, I'm going to get even! So you both better watch your backs! Because I HATE YOU! I HATE YOU! I HATE YOOOOU!!"

Tiffany angrily stomped her foot, splashing water everywhere.

Then she accidentally dropped her phone AGAIN and dove back into the water to find it.

OMG! Tiffany's video was even more CRAY-CRAY than MacKenzie's wacky bug video!

MacKenzie and I smiled at each other. And then in a surprising and unprecedented show of unity, we actually did the unthinkable. . . .

WAY TO GO!!

MACKENZIE AND ME,
GIVING EACH OTHER A HIGH FIVE!!

Tiffany was a selfie-addicted TYRANT! And
hopefully just the fact that we had that video
would make her think twice about retaliating.

Someone tapped me on my shoulder, and when I turned
around, I was surprised to see Patrick standing
behind me.

"WOW! Not only are Tiffany and her cell phone SOAKING WET, but it looks like her selfie club might be ALL WASHED UP too. Thanks to you!" He grinned.

"But my rep is ruined! Now there will be another nasty rumor that I'm so cruel I actually DROWNED a cell phone! So be afraid! Be VERY afraid!" I laughed.

"Well, I didn't want you to leave until I apologized for how everyone acted at lunch today. We were just disappointed that you weren't going to attend our meeting. We really appreciate you sticking up for us and helping to save our club. But things didn't work out like we'd planned," Patrick explained.

"No problem. Apology accepted. But, dude! It's about time you guys stopped playing with your lightsabers during meetings," I teased. "We're throwing that science club membership party tomorrow! And it's going to be a BLAST! So go round up the crew, and let's do this thing!"

☺!!

Today was my LAST day here at NHH, and my schedule was jam-packed.

Tiffany didn't say a single word to me all day. I'm guessing it's because I have a video of her confessing and having a meltdown in the school fountain. Even though her makeup was flawless, I'm pretty sure she doesn't want to put MY video on her fashion blog ☺!!

I think MacKenzie and I are now FRENEMIES! Which is a slight improvement over MORTAL ENEMIES who HATE each other's GUTS. But hey, at least it's progress!

Since Patrick and the rest of the crew are my friends, I decided that helping them save their science club was crucial.

We had agreed to meet at school an hour early to post sign-up sheets and put up posters to help generate excitement about joining our club.

187

I met Chase in the art room and was really
impressed with her posters. . . .

CHASE, YOUR POSTERS ARE AWESOME!

I was happy to see that our cool posters were getting a lot of attention in the halls.

My appointment to meet with Madame Danielle about the Paris trip was at noon, and I was a nervous wreck.

She started off by saying how much she'd enjoyed having me in her French class and that she'd heard a lot about me from other teachers, especially Mr. Winter.

I shuddered and braced myself for the news that I had been disqualified for the trip.

She said that Patrick and Sofia had met with Mr. Winter to explain that I hadn't stolen his lesson plan book and that, if anything, I would have immediately returned it to him.

He actually believed them since his book had been getting stolen for months before I'd arrived. So now Mr. Winter is recommending me for the trip, along with my French teacher from WCD!

Surprisingly, the meeting went really well. . . .

MADAME DANIELLE SAID SHE'D INFORM
STUDENTS OF HER DECISION ABOUT
THE TRIP TO PARIS IN THREE WEEKS!

She also explained that because of my art skills, she felt I would get even more out of the visit to the Louvre than most students.

So right now I'm really happy! In spite of my DISASTROUS week, I think I STILL have a really good chance of being awarded that trip to Paris!

SQUEEEEEE ☺!!

When the final bell rang, I rushed down to the science lab. The room was decorated with brightly colored balloons and the science club banner.

We had a table piled with food, and our music was blasting.

Although we were SUPERnervous, everything was finally ready.

I breathed a sigh of relief when we opened the classroom door and a long line of excited kids rushed inside. . . .

ME

Our science club membership drive party was a huge success!! Everyone LOVED our party favors! They were SUPERcool sunglasses that students got to keep.

And the cupcakes I had ordered from the CupCakery were absolutely DELISH!

Our ZANY music was lots of fun. And whenever our theme song, "She Blinded Me with Science," played, the entire room went NUTS!

OMG! Chase was such a great dancer. Sofia said she danced competitively and had won a ton of trophies.

We ended up with sixteen new members, for a total of twenty-two members! And, to show their appreciation, they gave me an honorary membership in the club! SQUEEEE ☺!!

When it was time to discuss club activities for next year, I couldn't help but make a joke. "Okay, all in favor of lightsaber fight scene reenactments from Star Wars movies, raise your right hand!" I said, all seriouslike.

Of course the only people to raise their hands were Patrick, Drake, Lee, and Mario.

"Okay! Now take your right hand and SLAP YOURSELF SILLY!" I joked.

Everybody in the room laughed really hard, including them. I think the guys got my point.

Soon it was time to say my good-byes, and we all hugged each other and agreed to stay in touch.

My week at North Hampton Hills had turned out better than I had imagined. But I was starting to worry that Tiffany's problem was possibly CONTAGIOUS. Why?

Because it was MY idea to take a CELEBRATORY SELFIE of me and the twenty-two members of the new-and-improved science club! I NEVER wanted to forget the wonderful time we had together being blinded by science!

!!

OMG! I can't believe I actually SURVIVED the student exchange program at North Hampton Hills International Academy!

SQUEEEEEEEE ☺!!

Even though the science club event was a huge success, my last few minutes at NHH turned into a complete DRAMAFEST! I had just finished cleaning out my locker and was on my way to the office to turn in my student ID when I noticed a large group of kids crowded around a locker in the west hall.

Since NHH's soccer team was playing in a tournament, quite a number of students had stayed after school for the game. Curious, I rushed down the hall to find out what was going on.

OMG, I immediately had a disgustingly freaky case of déjà vu. . . .

SOMEONE HAD VANDALIZED
A LOCKER WITH GRAFFITI!

The shocking thing was that those exact same words had been written on my WCD locker back in October.

My dad is a bug exterminator and works for my school, Westchester Country Day. He also arranged for me to attend there on a full scholarship.

Unfortunately, MacKenzie found out about my deep, dark secret and started taunting me.

So when someone scribbled BUG GIRL on MY locker in red lip gloss, MacKenzie was my FIRST and ONLY suspect.

But WHY would someone write "BUG GIRL" on a student's locker at NHH?

Once the distraught owner of the locker showed up, the crowd quickly scattered.

That's when the entire fiasco finally started to make sense. I was stunned to discover that the locker belonged to . . .

MACKENZIE, FREAKING OUT ABOUT
THE GRAFFITI ON HER LOCKER!

I immediately suspected Tiffany since she had
WARNED us to "watch our backs" in her angry
rant yesterday. And MacKenzie had admitted that
Tiffany had teased her about that video with the
BUG in her hair when she'd started attending NHH.

I felt SUPERsorry for MacKenzie since she was
obviously very upset. But I also couldn't help but
wonder if she remembered vandalizing MY locker
and writing those same cruel words.

MacKenzie was finally getting a taste of her OWN
medicine, and she totally deserved it.

However, her spiteful actions had also made me feel
hurt and alone. That's when I decided to be her
friend, not her frenemy.

"MacKenzie, are you okay? This is such a cruel and
disgusting prank!" I said. "I'm sorry you had to go
through this!"

MacKenzie slowly turned around to face me, with
tears streaming down her cheeks. . . .

MACKENZIE, ACCUSING ME OF
VANDALIZING HER LOCKER!

"Listen, MacKenzie!" I exclaimed. "I know you're angry right now. But I would NEVER stoop this low to hurt you or anyone else!"

"I don't believe you for one second! I think you came to NHH just to humiliate me!" MacKenzie screamed.

No matter how hard I tried to convince her that I was innocent, she refused to believe me.

Suddenly Tiffany appeared out of thin air.

"Hey, Nikki and MacKenzie, is something wrong? You two don't sound like BFFs anymore. OMG, MacKenzie! Did someone vandalize your locker? I wonder who HATES you that much?" she asked, batting her eyes all innocentlike. "Well, I'd love to hang out with you, but I gotta get back to that soccer tournament. Have fun!"

I definitely have to give Tiffany credit for being an evil genius. She'd probably heard one of the crazy rumors about how I'D vandalized MacKenzie's locker by writing "BUG GIRL" on it.

And actually doing the same thing to MacKenzie's NHH locker was the PERFECT setup!

Tiffany had effectively gotten even with MacKenzie and me by secretly launching World War III!!

Our new "friendship" had barely lasted twenty-four hours. And, ironically, now BOTH of us had been ridiculed as BUG GIRLS.

I just sighed and walked away.

Turning in my NHH student ID to the office was kind of bittersweet because I was already starting to miss my new friends.

But it also meant returning to my wonderful life at WCD and hanging out with cherished friends who adored me.

And OMG! I can hardly wait to get back there!

☺!!

SATURDAY, MAY 17—4:45 P.M.
IN MY BEDROOM

I was so physically and mentally exhausted from my week at NHH, I could have slept FOREVER!

I FINALLY dragged myself out of bed around noon, only because I had promised Brianna that I'd spend the afternoon in the kitchen helping her try to earn her cooking badge.

AGAIN ☹!!

I was eating lunch and skimming my mom's recipe book for quick and easy snacks when I got a text from Brandon:

> BRANDON: So, how was your week at Hogwarts? Luv the tacky uniforms (LOL)!

> NIKKI: It was good. Can't wait to get back to WCD. How was South Ridge?

BRANDON: We had fun hanging out with Max C. Definitely one cool dude. His lil' bro, Oliver, and Brianna are BFFs?

NIKKI: Yep! I'm trying to help her earn a cooking badge for Scouts. Any ideas for a super-EZ brat-proof snack?

BRANDON: How about caramel popcorn balls? Yummy too!

NIKKI: Popcorn balls?! Are you kidding me? Sounds way too complicated!

BRANDON: Nope. Super EZ! Even I can make them and I'm a cruddy cook. I made some last night.

NIKKI: Really?! What are the ingredients?

BRANDON: Just popcorn and caramel candy. Cooks in microwave.

NIKKI: That's all?! Very cool! Be
right back . . .

NIKKI: We have popcorn ☺! But no
caramel candy ☹!

BRANDON: I have a bag of candy.
Will bring it right over.

NIKKI: You're coming to my house?
NOW?!!

NIKKI: Brandon?

NIKKI: Hello? R U there?!

NIKKI: We'll just cook a PB & J
sandwich!

NIKKI: ?????? ☹!!

I was a little worried when Brandon disappeared like
that right in the middle of us texting each other.

About fifteen minutes later there was a knock on my front door. And when I opened it, Brandon was standing there holding a bag of caramels.

"You said you needed caramels, right?" He grinned. "And since I'm here, I'll share my secret recipe for popcorn balls and help out."

Brandon said his SUPEReasy recipe was only three steps: (1) melt twenty-eight caramel candies into a sauce with two tablespoons of water in the microwave, (2) cook one bag of popcorn, and (3) stir them together, shape into balls, and EAT!

He said it was an ingenious, foolproof recipe that he could make with his eyes closed. But was it Brianna-proof?

Brianna was excited about making popcorn balls! And Brandon and I were excited to be hanging out with each other after a long week apart. However, after Brandon prepared the sauce, Brianna got an attitude and started trying to boss everyone around. . . .

BRANDON AND ME, HELPING BRIANNA
MAKE POPCORN BALLS!

"Listen, Brianna, while Brandon stirs the caramel sauce, YOU get to microwave the popcorn. Doesn't that sound like FUN?!" I said cheerfully.

"NO! I WANNA STIR THE CARAMEL SAUCE!" She pouted.

"You're REALLY good at making popcorn. So that's going to be YOUR job," I said sternly.

I read the microwave popcorn box aloud. "Place ONE bag of popcorn in microwave. Set microwave to cook for FOUR minutes. Makes THREE servings."

"Okay, I'll make the STUPID popcorn!" Brianna finally muttered. "But as soon as I'm done, I'm gonna STIR the caramel sauce and TASTE it too! You're NOT the boss of ME!"

Then she stuck her tongue out at me. I was SUPERembarrassed that she was acting like such a BRAT in front of Brandon.

I handed Brianna the box of popcorn. "If you need any help, let me know."

Soon the caramel sauce was ready and cooling to room temperature and the popcorn was popping in the microwave. The sweet and savory aromas in the kitchen smelled delish!

Cooking with Brandon was actually kind of, um . . . ROMANTIC! SQUEEEEEEEE ☺!!

He stared at me and smiled, and I stared at him and smiled. All of this staring and smiling went on, like, FOREVER!

Until we were RUDELY interrupted by Brianna. She was gleefully stirring the caramel sauce and humming to herself. Suddenly she decided to sneak a taste and brought the huge bowl up to her mouth and tipped it sideways.

"Brianna! WHAT are you doing?!" I gasped. "Put that down right NOW before you accidentally—"

That's when Brianna said, "OOPS!!"

Brandon and I stared in horror as . . . SPLOOOSH!
The caramel sauce slowly poured down the front of her
shirt until she was covered in a huge, sticky MESS!

BRIANNA, IN A STICKY SITUATION

JUST GREAT ☹!! I grabbed some paper towels and was about to clean her up when I heard a ridiculously loud racket coming from the microwave.

POP-POP! POP-POP-POP! POP!
POP! POP-POP! POP-POP-POP!
POP-POP! POP! POP-POP! POP!
POP! POP-POP! POP-POP-POP!

"Why does it sound like July Fourth fireworks in there?" I asked, peering inside the microwave and noticing it was completely filled with popcorn. "Brianna, WHAT did you do?!!"

"I did exactly what YOU said. I put in FOUR bags for THREE minutes to make ONE serving!" she yelled at me.

"NOOO!! The directions said ONE bag for FOUR minutes to make THREE servings!" I groaned.

"OOPS!!" Brianna muttered again.

I hit the stop button and opened the door to the microwave. I was shocked and surprised when . . .

BRIANNA AND I ARE PRACTICALLY BURIED
ALIVE IN A HUGE AVALANCHE OF POPCORN!!

What a DISASTER! It took us an hour to clean up
the humongous MESS Brianna had made.

She DID try to help! But because she was still covered in sticky caramel, she just ended up a giant ball of popcorn and random kitchen stuff! . . .

BRIANNA, THE HUMAN POPCORN BALL!

But at least she was a SUPERyummy human
popcorn ball. . . .

BRIANNA SNACKS ON HERSELF!

Lucky for Brianna, Brandon had managed to save a cup of caramel sauce that was left over in the bowl, and I found a lot of popcorn still inside the microwave.

So Brianna was able to make a dozen mini popcorn balls, which she took to her Scout meeting later in the afternoon! . . .

BRIANNA'S MINI POPCORN BALLS

When Brianna got home, she excitedly explained how EVERYONE at her meeting LOVED her bite-size popcorn balls and begged for MORE!

Then she showed me her brand-new cooking badge! . . .

BRIANNA'S NEW COOKING BADGE

I congratulated my little sister and told her how proud I was of her that she had NOT given up.

Then I gave her a really big hug.

I was also proud of myself for being a mature, supportive, and patient big sister ☺!

UNTIL Brianna asked me to help her earn a gourmet chef badge. All she had to do was plan, prepare, and serve a formal four-course gourmet dinner for six people.

That's when I ran upstairs SCREAMING, locked myself in my bedroom, and hid in the back of my closet.

Sorry, but cooking with Brianna was a risky and dangerous activity, and, seriously, I would NEVER, EVER do it AGAIN ☹!!

Unless, of course, BRANDON was going to be Brianna's assistant chef!

SQUEEEEEE!!

☺!!!

<u>OMG!</u> I was SO happy to be back at WCD!
I wanted to KISS everything HELLO!

Like the walls, the floors, my locker, my textbooks,
and my very cute CRUSH, Brandon!

SQUEEEEEEE ☺!

Everyone shared exciting stories about the
schools they'd attended and the new friends
they'd made.

Like Brandon, Chloe and Zoey had enjoyed
attending South Ridge Middle School and hanging
out with Max C.

Of course I bragged about throwing a HUGE party
for my twenty-two new friends at NHH and showed
off the photos of the science club meeting.

Everyone was pretty impressed that I was such a social butterfly.

Anyway, my day was PERFECT! Until I got a very strange and ominous-sounding e-mail from Principal Winston:

Monday, May 19

TO: Nikki Maxwell

FROM: Principal Winston

RE: MacKenzie Hollister

Dear Nikki Maxwell,

This is to notify you that MacKenzie Hollister has requested an emergency meeting in my office on Tuesday, May 20, at 10:00 a.m. concerning a personal matter that involves you.

Please be prompt.

Thank you,

Principal Winston

220

JUST GREAT ☹!!

On Friday it was quite obvious that MacKenzie and Tiffany were still at war with each other.

But HOW did that involve ME at MY school?

I thought all the NHH drama had been resolved.

That's when I suddenly remembered MacKenzie's last day at WCD about a month ago.

She had threatened to file a phony complaint against me for cyberbullying her.

Only WHY would she do that NOW?!

I didn't know the answer, and it didn't really matter.

I was about to face my worst nightmare.

☹!!

TUESDAY, MAY 20—NOON
AT MY LOCKER

Today was my meeting with Principal Winston and MacKenzie, and I was a nervous wreck ☹!

"So, this is what I get for helping that drama queen get a bug out of her hair?" I fumed as I walked down to the office. "NEVER AGAIN!"

Back in April, one of MacKenzie's frenemies had secretly recorded her having a MELTDOWN about the bug in her hair and then texted the video to a few friends.

The video got circulated around the entire school, and one day during lunch MacKenzie caught her CCP friends watching it and laughing behind her back.

MacKenzie was so angry and humiliated, she stopped being friends with her BFF, Jessica, and demanded that her parents let her transfer to a new school.

When they refused, MacKenzie decided to take matters into her own hands. She secretly posted a copy of her own bug video on YouTube. . . .

MACKENZIE POSTS
HER BUG VIDEO ONLINE!

MacKenzie LIED and told her parents that the situation had escalated into a more serious one because Nikki Maxwell (ME?!) had posted the video online and was cyberbullying her.

Then she pleaded with her parents to transfer her to North Hampton Hills International Academy!

After her FAKE meltdown, complete with hysterical crying worthy of an Academy Award, her concerned parents relented and agreed to send her to a new school.

It's sad, but true! MacKenzie Hollister is such a cruel and malicious person that she had heartlessly cyberbullied HERSELF!

Anyway, when I arrived at the office for our meeting this morning, MacKenzie was already there, applying her lip gloss. The secretary was on her lunch break, and Principal Winston's door was closed.

"Hi, MacKenzie!" I said awkwardly.

She glared at me like I was something large, green, and slimy that she'd just sneezed into a tissue.

I decided to try to reason with her one last time.

"Why are you doing this, MacKenzie?! It makes no sense at all!"

"Actually, I have TWO very good reasons! First, if you're expelled for cyberbullying, then everyone at NHH will believe that I was telling the truth and YOU were lying. Second, Tiffany now HATES you as much as I do, especially since you undermined her beloved selfie club. Once I've FINALLY gotten even with you, she'll totally ADORE me and we'll become BFFs!"

"You'd actually TRUST Tiffany to be your BFF?!"

"Of course NOT! I'll just PRETEND to be her BFF . . . until I stab her in the back, label her an uncool, selfie-addicted weirdo, turn all her friends against her, AND steal her title as QUEEN BEE! It's all part of my carefully crafted master plan!"

"So, let me get this straight, MacKenzie. You'd LIE about me and completely DESTROY my life just to hang out with a popular girl at NHH?!"

"ABSOLUTELY! But don't take it personally, hon! I realize all of this is probably MY fault. But you have no idea how STRESSFUL and HUMILIATING it was to have that huge, icky BUG stuck in my hair."

It was quite obvious that this girl was out of touch with reality AND more SELF-ABSORBED than a SPONGE the size of New Jersey!

"Sorry, MacKenzie! But as someone who's been a real victim of cyberbullying—thanks to YOU, by the way—I have some invaluable advice for you. GET OVER IT!!!"

"I will. As soon as you're EXPELLED!!" She sneered. "All I have to do is convince that clueless slob, Principal Winston, that you're guilty. He'll believe anything I say!"

I watched in disbelief as MacKenzie took a mirror out of her purse and actually practiced her CRY FACE!

"Principal Winston!" she fake sobbed. "Nikki's bullied me, and it's been horrible! I saw her post that video with my own eyes! Please HELP me!! . . ."

NIKKI IS A MONSTER!!

MACKENZIE, PRACTICING FAKE CRYING

"And YOU'RE a pathological LIAR!" I shot back.

"You say that like it's a BAD thing!" She grinned.

Suddenly the office door opened and a lady wearing trendy, cute clothes entered with a cameraman in tow.

MacKenzie and I exchanged curious looks.

"What did you do, MacKenzie?! Contact a national NEWS network?!" I complained.

"No! I didn't," she replied. "I have no idea what they're here for."

"Excuse me! Do you girls have a minute?" the reporter asked. "We're with TeenTV News!"

"TeenTV?!" MacKenzie shrieked. "Are you going to be filming here at the school? If so, I need to put on my high-definition lip gloss!"

"Well, that depends," the reporter answered. "We're here to find out more about a video that was posted online on April 21. It was about a girl with a bug stuck in her—"

"OMG, Nikki! You sent that humiliating bug video to TeenTV?!" MacKenzie shrieked. "Why are you trying to RUIN my life?! I'll just lock myself inside the office supply closet until they leave."

Then she very rudely SHOVED me toward the reporter.

"Interview HER. It's ALL her fault. But be careful. She's so UGLY she might BREAK your camera!" MacKenzie sneered.

"SHOVE me like that again, girlfriend, and you'll see just how UGLY I can get!" I fumed.

But I just said that inside my head, so no one else heard it but me.

Since the school secretary was still at lunch, Mr. Winston was in his office, and MacKenzie had pretty much barricaded herself inside the office supply closet, I sighed and reluctantly agreed to talk to the reporter.

"We're looking for a student named Nikki Maxwell," the reporter said. "Do you know her? When we called here yesterday, we were given her name by a student office assistant named Jessica."

"Actually, she is ME! I mean, me is HER! What I'm trying to say is, I'M Nikki Maxwell," I babbled incoherently.

"Fabulous!" she replied. "Ready to film, Steve!" she cued her cameraman. "This is Jade Santana, coming to you live with a *TeenTV News* exclusive!"

Even though I was on television a few months ago (it's a long story and another diary!), I fidgeted uncomfortably and smiled awkwardly into the camera.

I had to restrain myself from grabbing the nearest wastebasket, shoving it over my head, and running out of the office SCREAMING!

The reporter continued. "I'm here with Nikki Maxwell, the mastermind and creator of the VIRAL video that is sweeping TeenTV and the nation . . . the STINK BUG SHAKE!" Jade exclaimed. "Congratulations, Nikki! You've just been nominated for the TeenTV Awesome Awards Best Viral Video of the Year!! How do you feel?"

That's when the office supply closet door slowly opened.

A very shocked and surprised MacKenzie cautiously peeked out.

"How do I feel? Um . . . REALLY confused!" I muttered. "Can you run all of that by me again, please? I'm not sure I understood everything you just said!"

"Well, Nikki, the teens of the world have spoken. And they LOVE your video!" Jade exclaimed. "Did you have any idea it was going to go viral?"

ME, BEING INTERVIEWED BY TEENTV FOR
BEST VIRAL VIDEO OF THE YEAR!!

Suddenly my interview with Jade was RUDELY interrupted.

"STOP! You should be interviewing ME, not HER!!" MacKenzie screeched as she jumped in front of me. "I'M the REAL STAR of that video!"

Then she got really close to the camera and did a DUCK FACE. That girl was a hot mess!

"Sorry! But WHO are you again?" Jade frowned.

"MACKENZIE HOLLISTER! I'M the one who posted that viral video of—what did you call it—the Stink Bug Shake that's sweeping the nation! NOT this pathetic POSEUR!" she said, pointing at me.

"Wait a minute, MacKenzie! For the past month, you've been spreading nasty rumors and telling EVERYONE that I posted that bug video!" I exclaimed. "So NOW you're CHANGING your story?!"

"Nikki, do you actually think I'M going to STUPIDLY stand by and let YOU take credit for all of MY hard work?!" MacKenzie shrieked. "GIRL, BYE!"

Jade and the cameraman exchanged puzzled glances. "Listen, girls, you're going to have to figure all of this out and do it quickly. We're going live to finish this segment in sixty, no, fifty seconds!" Jade said, looking at her watch.

I couldn't believe I FINALLY had a chance to END this NIGHTMARE once and for all.

"So, let me get this straight, MacKenzie! You're willing to admit on national television that YOU purposely put that video online and I had absolutely nothing to do with it?" I asked.

"YES! You got it straight!" she snarled. "Just admit it! You WISH you had BUGS in your hair like I do. This is MY moment! Quit trying to steal it, you basic, no-talent WANNABE!"

"Hello, I'm Jade, and we're back live for TeenTV! So, MacKenzie, tell us how you first came up with the concept for your fabulous video?" . . .

MACKENZIE, BEING INTERVIEWED BY
TEENTV ABOUT HER VIRAL VIDEO!

"When you're a trained dance GENIUS like I am, it all comes naturally! One day I was cleaning the girls' locker room showers when an idea just, um . . . crawled into my head. And then later, in class, it tangled itself in my hair and, um . . . became inspiration. It actually made me cry. Tears of joy! And then, to express the emotional rawness I was feeling, I started to scream! And jump around too! Then I actually projectile vomited, um . . . passion! I just had to get my video out there and share it with the world, so I posted it. And, Jade, the rest is history!" MacKenzie raved overdramatically.

I could NOT believe that girl had just confessed on national TV! I breathed a sigh of relief as I continued to watch the MacKenzie freak show.

"So, what are your future plans?!" Jade asked.

"Well, I'm open to guest appearances on all the most popular dance TV shows. My vision is to revolutionize the Internet with my cutting-edge dance art, and I think I'm on my way to accomplishing that!"

"OMG! That was SO deep!" Jade gushed. "So, can you tell us which performance artist has inspired you the most?"

"NONE of them! Most performance artists are inspired by ME!" MacKenzie bragged.

Maybe the glare from those bright camera lights had affected my eyes. But while I was watching MacKenzie's interview, her head appeared to be swelling up larger and larger!

OMG! Her EGO was so big, it had stretch marks.

I was just hoping she'd complete her interview before her head actually EXPLODED on live television!

BOOOM!!

After the TeenTV interview was over, students excitedly swarmed the halls and actually mobbed MacKenzie. . . .

MACKENZIE'S FAN CLUB

They begged her for an autograph and took selfies with her like she was a Hollywood A-list celebrity or something.

Due to MacKenzie's newfound FAME, she decided to CANCEL the meeting with Principal Winston!!

Which means I no longer have to worry about getting kicked out of school because of false allegations of cyberbullying. Since MacKenzie just confessed on national television that SHE posted the bug video, this DRAMAFEST is over!

FOREVER!!

SQUEEEEEE!!

☺!!

OMG! I feel SO relieved! It's like a ton of weight has FINALLY been lifted off my shoulders.

I actually survived the student exchange program at North Hampton Hills.

I'm STILL in the running for that fabulous trip to Paris.

That selfie-addicted DIVA, Tiffany Blaine Davenport, is out of my life FOREVER!

And MacKenzie's cyberbullying FIASCO is finally over.

But when Chloe, Zoey, and I passed by the office after lunch today, we saw the STRANGEST thing.

MacKenzie was frantically digging through the lost and found box like she'd lost her MIND! And Jessica was helping her. . . .

MACKENZIE SEARCHES FOR
HER LOST DIARY!

That's when I remembered that she'd LOST her leopard-print diary and NEVER found it. Which was actually MY DIARY, which she'd STOLEN from ME and disguised with a leopard-print cover (another LONG story)! At least I got it back!

Anyway, it's official! MacKenzie announced that she's transferring from NHH BACK to WCD!

I think this probably means she HATES me LESS than she HATES Tiffany.

And since her video went viral, she has resumed her throne as queen of the CCPs.

According to the latest gossip, MacKenzie and Jessica are BFFs again. They're already planning to make a Part Two of the bug video.

Unfortunately for me, MacKenzie was reassigned to the locker right next to MINE.

JUST GREAT ☹!!

MacKenzie was gone for FIVE weeks and has only been back for a few hours.

But it feels like she never LEFT!

I really hope her experiences at North Hampton Hills International Academy taught her a valuable lesson and that she'll change for the better.

But personally . . . I wouldn't hold my BREATH ☹!

I'm just happy to be back at WCD and hanging out with my friends, Chloe, Zoey, and Brandon.

And although MY life is far from perfect, I'm REALLY happy to FINALLY have it back.

WHY? Because . . .

I'm SUCH a DORK!!

☺!!

Nikki is completely crushing on Brandon, and nothing or **NO ONE** can change that. Can they? New boy André certainly thinks he can.

Who will Nikki choose?

Find out in

CRUSH CATASTROPHE . . .

WEDNESDAY, MAY 21—7:15 A.M.
AT HOME

SQUEEEEEE ☺!! I think I'm suffering from a severe case of CRUSH-ITIS!!

OMG! I wonder if I'm actually falling in . . .

. . . because I feel so INSANELY happy, I could VOMIT sunshine, rainbows, confetti, glitter, and those cute little Skittles candy thingies! My heart is pounding, my palms are sweaty, and the butterflies fluttering around inside my stomach are making me feel a little queasy.

247

Unfortunately, there is no known CURE. . . .

MY CRUSH-ITIS DIAGNOSIS

How I got this acute case of crush-itis is kind of a long and complicated story. I was just about to eat breakfast and head off to school. . . .

251

254

ME, SCOLDING DAISY
FOR BEING A VERY BAD DOG!

I can't believe Daisy is actually a SNEAKY SAUSAGE SNATCHER. But hey! She's MY adorable little sneaky sausage snatcher!

257

I just could NOT understand how something so small, cute, and cuddly could completely TRASH our home in less than three minutes.

There is just ONE major difference between Daisy and my bratty little sister, Brianna.

Brianna is supposed to go potty INSIDE but sometimes has accidents OUTSIDE! And Daisy is supposed to go potty OUTSIDE but sometimes has accidents INSIDE!

I had barely started cleaning up the huge mess Daisy had made when I had to rush her outside to use the bathroom.

Afterward, she waded through a mud puddle and then playfully jumped all over me.

OMG! It looked like Daisy and I had been in a mud-wrestling match. And I had LOST ☹!

I was desperately trying to drag her back into the house when I unexpectedly ran into . . .

OMG! I was SO embarrassed.

I was completely covered in Daisy's muddy paw prints, from head to toe. I wanted to open our mailbox, climb inside it, and DIE!!

Brandon's eyes twinkled as he bit his lower lip. It was quite obvious he was trying his best not to further HUMILIATE me by laughing.

"Um . . . are you okay?" he asked.

"Sure, everything's . . . fine, actually. Daisy and I were just taking a little walk, and . . ."

"Let me guess. You decided to roll around in a mud puddle?" Brandon grinned.

I couldn't help rolling my eyes at him.

Brandon explained that he was up early delivering material to the person designing a donation website for Fuzzy Friends Animal Rescue Center, where he volunteers.

Daisy happily wagged her tail and stared at Brandon like he was a human-sized doggie snack. He scooped her up and laughed. . . .

HELLO, DAISY! HAVE YOU BEEN GIVING POOR NIKKI A REALLY HARD TIME? YES?!

BARK!!

BRANDON, CHATTING WITH DAISY

That's when I told him about all the mischief that Daisy had gotten into.

"Brandon, I'm completely exhausted, and I just got out of bed an hour ago. If Daisy was a toy dog, I swear I'd take out her batteries and throw them away!" I grumbled.

"That's too bad. Hey, maybe some obedience training will solve your problem!" Brandon said.

"Thanks for the advice. But obedience training sounds SUPERintense. I barely make it through the TEN minutes of warm-up exercises in PE class," I muttered in frustration.

"Actually, the obedience training is for DAISY. Not YOU!" Brandon laughed. "I'm very sure YOU don't eat out of the garbage or drink out of the toilet. Right?!"

I just stared at Brandon in shock. I could NOT believe he'd actually asked me such a PERSONAL question. How RUDE!!

That's when I started to wonder if Brianna had been gossiping about me to Brandon behind my back.

I would NEVER, EVER eat out of the GARBAGE! EWW ☹!

Well, unless I had a REALLY good reason.

Like the time Brianna accidentally threw away the little white bag that contained my double-chocolate, double-fudge cupcake.

I'd actually JUST purchased it from the CupCakery.

YES! I'll admit I had to dig through the garbage to find it.

And there was a big blob of jelly, a half-eaten fish stick, and slimy oatmeal stuck to the outside of the bag that looked pretty nasty.

But the cupcake inside seemed okay, so I actually ATE it. . . .

YUM!

ME, EATING OUT OF THE GARBAGE!

I would NEVER, EVER drink anything as gross as TOILET water! EWW ☹!

Well, I wouldn't drink it on purpose, anyway.

A few weeks ago Brianna's teddy bear, Hans, accidentally fell into the toilet. A gallon of toilet water splashed all over me while I was screaming. . . .

ME, SWALLOWING TOILET WATER!

But I DIDN'T have my head stuck inside the toilet bowl, GUZZLING the water like I was dying of thirst or something.

I didn't tell Brandon about the garbage or the toilet water because then he'd think I needed doggie obedience training ALONG with Daisy ☹!

Sorry! But I'm a VERY private person, and I don't like putting my business in the streets!

Finally he changed the subject. Thank goodness!

"Listen, Nikki! I have an idea. I'd be happy to train Daisy. We can do two sessions a week, right in your backyard."

"That sounds FANTASTIC!" I exclaimed. "How about Wednesdays and Saturdays, starting this Saturday?"

"No problem! I'm really looking forward to us hanging out. It's going to be fun!"

"Well, Daisy loves hanging out with YOU!" I said.

That's when Brandon STARED right into the . . . murky depths of my . . . inner soul. Then he smiled kind of shy-like and brushed his shaggy bangs out of his eyes. I thought I was going to MELT!

"Actually, I'm looking forward to hanging out with YOU. Not your DOG!" He blushed. . . .

YES! Brandon actually said those words to me!

SQUEEEEEE ☺!

At that very moment, CRUSH-ITIS hit me!

Like a TON of bricks! . . .

ME, BEING HIT WITH CRUSH-ITIS!

"Um, same here, Brandon," I giggled nervously. "We're going to have a blast! And by 'we,' I mean YOU and I. Not my DOG."

"COOL!" Brandon said as he gave me a crooked smile.

"VERY COOL!" I blushed.

Then I took several deep breaths and tried to calm the butterflies fluttering in my slightly queasy stomach.

WHY?

Because I was VERY sure Brandon would CANCEL the dog training sessions and REFUSE to hang out with me if I started PUKING butterflies on the sidewalk!

Like, WHO does THAT?!!

Only a complete WEIRDO!!

We both just stood there awkwardly smiling at each other for what seemed like FOREVER!!

Since Brandon had agreed to help me with Daisy, I volunteered to help him with his Fuzzy Friends website project.

He was so happy, he grinned from ear to ear.

So I'll be drawing cute artwork for the website, which we'll be working on mostly at school.

I think Brandon and me spending more time together is a great idea!

Hopefully, we'll become even better friends than we already are.

He likes me a lot and I like him a lot, so WHAT could possibly go WRONG?!

Sorry! But I REFUSE to let anything or anybody RUIN our very special FRIENDSHIP!

Anyway, I really need to stop writing. School starts in less than thirty minutes! And I STILL need to finish cleaning the house and change out of my muddy clothes.

OMG! If my MOM came home from work and saw the HUGE MESS Daisy made, she'd have a complete MELTDOWN.

She'd drop Daisy and me off at Fuzzy Friends . . .

. . . TO BE ADOPTED BY A NEW FAMILY!!

I can't wait to tell my BFFs, Chloe and Zoey, the very exciting news that Brandon and I will be hanging out together training Daisy AND working on his Fuzzy Friends project.

And since Chloe reads a lot of teen romance and Zoey is into self-help books, I'm sure they'll give me advice on how to deal with my CRUSH-ITIS!

WOW! I just had the STRANGEST thought! I wonder if it's CONTAGIOUS?! . . .

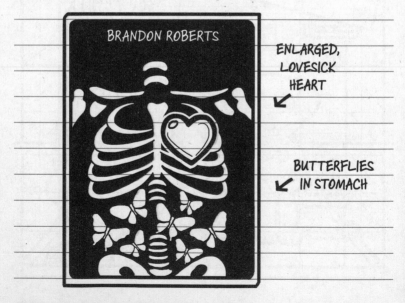

BRANDON ROBERTS

ENLARGED, LOVESICK HEART

BUTTERFLIES IN STOMACH

YOU NEVER KNOW!! ☺!!

THURSDAY, MAY 22—9:45 A.M.
AT MY LOCKER

Yesterday during lunch I confided in Chloe and Zoey about my crush-itis and everything that had happened between Brandon and me.

They were VERY supportive and gave me a great big HUG! . . .

CHLOE, ZOEY, AND I DO A GROUP HUG!!

"Nikki, you have more ISSUES than a two-year subscription to Seventeen magazine!" Chloe teased.

"But we still LOVE you!" Zoey giggled.

Chloe and Zoey are practically EXPERTS on teen romance and gave me some awesome advice. . . .

First of all, a CRUSH can be a noun (the PERSON you're obsessed with) or a verb (having warm-'n'-fuzzy FEELINGS for that person). Which means you can CRUSH on your CRUSH ☺!

It's also perfectly normal to feel NERVOUS and a little AWKWARD around your crush.

Heck, I get NERVOUS just THINKING ABOUT how NERVOUS Brandon makes me feel!

But here's the really crazy part. Because you're a NERVOUS WRECK, you'll often SAY and DO incredibly STUPID and EMBARRASSING things that make your crush-itis even WORSE. . . .

HOW TO COMPLETELY HUMILIATE YOURSELF IN FRONT OF YOUR CRUSH!

The GOOD NEWS is that the whole crush thing is mostly just harmless fun ☺! Your crush will probably NEVER even know you're actually crushing on 'em.

But the BAD NEWS is that even the mildest crush can potentially evolve into a CRUSH-ITIS CRISIS! And when that happens, you could possibly LOSE. YOUR. MIND!! . . .

A CLASSIC CRUSH ESCALATING INTO A CRUSH-ITIS CRISIS!

The SCARIEST part for me is that if my crush-itis gets worse, I could end up missing school!

And what if it gets to the point where I have to stay in BED the ENTIRE summer?!

I wouldn't be able to do anything except . . .

1. daydream about my crush

2. doodle pictures of my crush

3. listen to music that reminds me of my crush

AND

4. write in my diary about my crush.

Suddenly I realized just how SERIOUS my situation was.

"OMG! Chloe and Zoey! I could end up bedridden and suffering from CRUSH-ITIS for the rest of my LIFE!!" . . .

ME, FEELING INSANELY HAPPY AND WISHING
THAT MY CRUSH-ITIS LASTS FOREVER!!

278

But the most important thing I need to remember is that the excitement of most crushes simply fizzles out over time when you start to mature and/or finally realize your KNIGHT in shining ARMOR is really a LOSER in ALUMINUM FOIL!

Okay, I'm VERY sure that Brandon is NOT a LOSER in ALUMINUM FOIL. But I understand the point.

Chloe and Zoey assured me that Brandon is a really nice guy and I am going to be just fine.

So I'll take their advice and try not to worry or stress out about the situation.

Although, I must admit, having those cute little butterfly thingies in my stomach kind of

TICKLES!

We finally finished our lunch, and then my BFFs did the SWEETEST thing. They treated me to an extra-large HOT FUDGE BROWNIE SUNDAE from the snack bar!

And when I asked why they were being so kind to me, Zoey broke into giggles and exclaimed . . .

"Actually, we're saving all our money for our summer tour. And buying you ice cream is CHEAPER than THERAPY!!"

You gotta LOVE 'em!!

☺!

FRIDAY, MAY 23—2:30 P.M.
AT MY LOCKER

I can't believe school will be over in a little more than a week. SQUEEEEEEEE ☺!!

Even though the entire year has been a nonstop DRAMAFEST, it actually went by pretty fast.

Summer vacation is going to be a total BLAST!!

In July my band, Actually, I'm Not Really Sure Yet, will be doing a monthlong national tour as the opening act for the superstar boy band . . .

How COOL and EXCITING will that be ☺?!!

Trevor Chase, the world-famous producer, has asked me to put together a thirty-minute show that includes our original song "Dorks Rule!"

We'll officially start band rehearsals again after the school year ends. OMG! I can't even imagine going on a national tour with BRANDON ☺! And the rest of my band members too!

Chloe and Zoey are SUPERexcited about our tour and have been talking about it nonstop. They also plan to post videos on YouTube of their tour adventures in hopes of landing their own reality TV show.

They already have a name for their project: *Chloe and Zoey: Teens on Tour!*

As their BFF, the LAST thing I wanted was to discourage them from pursuing their dream of having a TV show.

But after doing my own show back in March, I am so OVER reality TV! . . .

ME, FREAKING OUT ABOUT
THE TV CAMERAS EVERYWHERE ☹!

I'm helping Chloe and Zoey brainstorm ideas for
their show, and I'll try to be supportive of them
from BEHIND the camera.

I ALSO applied for a scholarship to study abroad in PARIS, FRANCE, this summer ☺!

OMG! Can you imagine ME touring the city and hanging out at the famous Louvre art museum? . . .

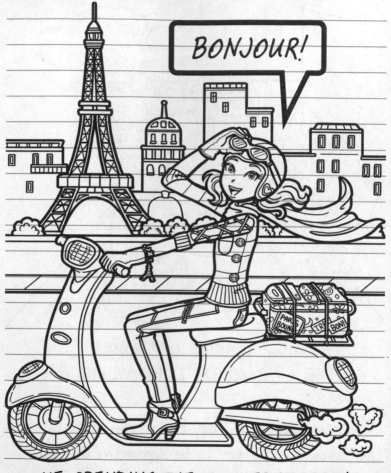

ME, SPENDING THE SUMMER IN PARIS!

I know! To be honest, NEITHER can I ☹!

So I'm definitely NOT going to sit around holding my BREATH, waiting for a FANTASY SUMMER IN PARIS to happen. WHY? Because LIFE is NOT a romantic comedy movie!

The BIGGEST milestone for me will be that in the fall, I'll FINALLY be starting . . .

HIGH SCHOOL ☺!!

YES!! I'll actually be a FRESHMAN!

High school kids are so COOL. And very MATURE. And really SOPHISTICATED! The BEST thing is that they're old enough to get a DRIVER'S LICENSE!

OMG! Can you imagine Chloe, Zoey, and me driving to school together EVERY. SINGLE. DAY?!

And since we'll be in HIGH SCHOOL, we'll be very cool, mature, and sophisticated TOO!!

I bet we'll be so different then that we'll BARELY recognize ourselves in the mirror! Or in a really CUTE hot pink sporty convertible! . . .

CHLOE, ZOEY, AND ME IN HIGH SCHOOL!

The best thing about high school is that I WON'T have a locker next to MacKenzie Hollister anymore. Thank goodness ☺!

Did I mention that MacKenzie transferred from North Hampton Hills BACK to Westchester Country Day on Tuesday?!

YEP!! Just like the scary villain in a horror movie . . . SHE'S BAAAAAACK!!

Yesterday I overheard MacKenzie actually BRAGGING to her friends that some NHH students had asked why she was leaving after barely a month and she'd answered them smugly . . .

"I've lied, gossiped, backstabbed, started nasty rumors, destroyed reputations, and created chaos. My work HERE is DONE!"

I mean, WHO says stuff like that? Only a self-absorbed, psychotic . . .

SOCIOPATH!!

Calling MacKenzie a MEAN GIRL is an understatement. She's PURE EVIL in hair extensions and sparkly nail polish.

When life gives MacKenzie LEMONS, she MALICIOUSLY squirts the juice in other people's EYES! . . .

MACKENZIE SHOWS OFF HER SKILLZ WITH FRESH LEMONS!

I had just arrived at my first-hour class when I was handed a note from the OFFICE.

Of course I was VERY worried. MacKenzie had recently tried to get me kicked out of school on a phony allegation of cyberbullying. It was very possible that she was stirring up MORE drama.

Or maybe the school janitor had FINALLY figured out that my BFFs and I had been SECRETLY hanging out in his janitor's closet for the past NINE MONTHS.

We could be facing a week of detention ☹!

Anyway, after talking to the secretary, I received some surprising news.

Our school is hosting students for another week of the student exchange program with local schools, and I've been drafted to be a student ambassador. JUST GREAT ☹!

I actually participated in this SAME program a week ago at North Hampton Hills International Academy. It was supposed to be the last week, but apparently the program was so popular that it was extended so more kids from other schools could participate.

Unfortunately, my student ambassador was a

selfie-addicted drama queen named Tiffany.

OMG! The girl was TREACHEROUS! She made MacKenzie look like Dora the Explorer! . . .

TIFFANY VANDALIZES MACKENZIE'S LOCKER AND FRAMES ME FOR IT!!

I'd LOVE to tell you all the dirty details, but THAT is another DIARY.

Anyway, the secretary said my participation as a student ambassador is MANDATORY! So I don't have a choice in the matter ☹!

She said all I have to do is be friendly and escort the student to all my classes, starting on Monday.

However, due to class sizes, she temporarily switched the times of my PE class and library hour, and gave me an earlier lunch period. So it looks like I probably won't be seeing much of Chloe and Zoey next week ☹.

This totally STINKS because I've ALREADY made plans next week to spend what little spare time I have at school helping Brandon with his Fuzzy Friends website, planning our concert tour, and brainstorming ideas with Chloe and Zoey for their video project.

Anyway, the school secretary told me the exchange student's name and gave me an e-mail address.

I think she said it was Angie.

No, it was . . . Andrea.

I think.

I just hope she's nice.

Between the exchange student, Daisy's training, Brandon's Fuzzy Friends project, the summer tour, AND my BFFs' YouTube videos, my schedule for the end of school is going to be . . .

BRUTAL ☹!!

But, luckily, my CRUSH and BFFs are very understanding and SUPERsupportive!

So WHAT could possibly go WRONG?!

☺!!

IN MY BEDROOM

Chloe and Zoey came over after school. We ordered pizza and hung out.

I confessed to my BFFs that after all the senseless DRAMA with Tiffany at NHH, I was a little worried about spending an entire week with Andrea.

I mean, WHAT if Tiffany and Andrea were friends?!

Andrea could be a selfie-addicted drama queen too!

Chloe and Zoey came up with an idea that was pure GENIUS!

They said it might help if I sent a friendly e-mail to Andrea introducing myself BEFORE we officially meet on Monday.

So that's exactly what I did. . . .

* * * * * * * * * * * * * * * *

Hi,

My name is Nikki, and I'm going to be your student
ambassador at Westchester Country Day. I'm
looking forward to meeting you on Monday. If
you have any questions, just let me know and I'll
be happy to answer them (as long as they're NOT
about geometry homework). Take care ☺!

Nikki

* * * * * * * * * * * * * * * *

As soon as I hit the send button, I immediately
started to have second thoughts.

What if Andrea thought my e-mail was silly and
that I was really immature for my age ☹?!

I was surprised when about fifteen minutes later
an e-mail from Andrea popped into my inbox. Wow!
That was FAST!

* * * * * * * * * * * * * *

Hi, Nikki,

Thanks for the e-mail. I'm really looking forward to
meeting you, too.

To be quite honest, I'm a little nervous about
spending the week at WCD. And I'm even more
nervous about pop quizzes in geometry!

Any advice or tips you could give me about fitting
in at WCD and NOT completely HUMILIATING
myself would be greatly appreciated.

A-

* * * * * * * * * * * * * *

Hi, A-,

Don't worry! Like at most schools, the majority of
students at WCD are pretty nice. Just avoid the
mean girls and the super-annoying guys and you'll

295

be fine. None of the guys have made fun of my
hairy legs. Lately 😊!

I can't wait for you to meet my BFFs, Chloe and
Zoey. And Brandon, too. He's my crush and a
TOTAL CUTIE! You can just call us Branikki! But
PLEASE don't tell him I said that (LOL). We'll all be
hanging out together. It's going to be fun 😊!

Nikki

* * * * * * * * * * * * * *

Hi, Nikki,

Thanks for the advice. I feel a lot better already. I'm
glad you're my student ambassador.

I just transferred to NHH a few weeks ago, so I
haven't made any friends here yet. You're lucky to
have friends like Chloe, Zoey, and Brandon. I can't
wait to meet all of you.

A-

* * * * * * * * * * * * * * * *

Hi, A-,

Being the new kid totally sucks! Been there, done that, got the T-shirt!

I was recently at NHH for this same program, so we may have even passed each other in the halls. I met some nice kids there and made a lot of new friends. You should definitely consider joining the NHH Science Club! We'll talk more when you get here. Have a great weekend 😊!

Nikki

* * * * * * * * * * * * * * *

Chloe and Zoey's idea worked like a charm!

After our e-mails, it almost feels like Andrea and I already know each other.

She seems really nice and has a wacky sense of humor.

297

I can't wait to introduce her to the NHH Science Club members.

To give Andrea a really warm welcome, I came up with the COOLEST idea.

I made a welcome sign out of hot pink glitter.

I think she's going to LOVE it! . . .

WELCOME, ANDREA, TO WCD!!

Well, at least Andrea is NOT a self-absorbed, psychotic SOCIOPATH (like some people I know).

Okay, I'll admit I was wrong!

It looks like this student ambassador thing is NOT going to be a major PAIN IN THE BEHIND after all.

It's going to be FUN!

And I might end up making a REALLY good friend!

☺!!

Today was Daisy's first doggie obedience session with Brandon, and I could hardly wait.

Since he volunteers several times a week at Fuzzy Friends, he's an excellent dog trainer. I had no doubt that very soon Daisy was going to be the best-trained dog in the entire city.

I was even thinking about entering her in one of those SUPERfancy dog shows. You know, where snobby people prance around with their snobby dogs in front of a snobby judge and the winner gets a big trophy.

In a few months, THAT could be US!

SQUEEEEEEEE ☺!

And Brandon will there with Daisy and me to capture it all. . . .

DAISY WINS BEST IN SHOW!!

Daisy and I sat in the backyard and listened carefully as Brandon enthusiastically explained her first lesson. . . .

DAISY'S FIRST TRAINING SESSION
WITH BRANDON!

First Brandon attached the leash to Daisy's collar.

Then, to get her to walk, he offered her a doggie treat from a few feet away.

My job was to walk slowly around the yard with Daisy on the leash as she followed Brandon and his treats.

If Daisy calmly followed him, he praised her and rewarded her with more treats.

However, if she got distracted or started pulling on the leash, I'd stand firmly in place until she stopped misbehaving.

Daisy caught on really fast.

And soon she was walking around the backyard on her leash like a pro.

Until she got bored and decided it would be more fun to hang out with a SQUIRREL. . . .

DAISY, TRYING TO MAKE FRIENDS
WITH A SQUIRREL

My silly dog chased that squirrel around and around in circles until . . .

BRANDON AND I FOUND OURSELVES
A LITTLE, UM . . . TANGLED UP!!

"BAD DOG, DAISY! BAD DOG!" I yelled.

"NO, DAISY! NO!" Brandon said, reprimanding her sternly.

But she just sat there, staring at us all innocent-like with her big brown puppy-dog eyes, pretending she didn't have the slightest idea how we'd gotten all tied up like that.

OMG!

It was so EMBARRASSING!

And EXCITING!

And FUN!

And kind of ROMANTIC!

We couldn't help but laugh at how ridiculous we looked as we tried to untangle ourselves from Daisy's leash.

In spite of the squirrel FIASCO, we both agreed that Daisy is a smart dog and had successfully learned to walk on a leash.

At our next session Brandon will be teaching Daisy the sit and stay commands.

I just hope it will be as ~~fun and romantic~~ interesting and educational as today's lesson was.

SQUEEEEEE!!

☺!!

SATURDAY—3:00 P.M.
IN MY BEDROOM

After Brandon left, I decided to finish up my history homework.

I was in my bedroom when someone knocked on my door. I assumed it was Brianna.

"No, Brianna! You can't play the Princess Sugar Plum video game on my cell phone!" I yelled. "I'm doing my homework!"

My dad opened the door and stuck his head in. "Nikki, it's me. I need to be on the social medium," he announced. "Can you help me?"

"The social medium? Dad, what are you talking about?!" I asked.

"You know, the Instachat, the Snapgram, the Facefriends, and Tweetering! I want it all for my business, Maxwell's Bug Extermination!" he said, sitting down on my bed. UNINVITED!! . . .

My mom is on Facebook, keeping up with her high school friends and embarrassing ME by posting UNAUTHORIZED photos.

But my dad? He still listens to baseball games on an old-school, battery-operated BOOM BOX.

"I need to be on the Interweb, er, I mean, INTERNET, to get more business," he explained. "I want to sign up for all those popular sites, like Bookface and Instagrammy. I need to be connected and keep my finger on the pulse of the youth."

The way my dad had MURDERED the names of all those social media sites, I doubted there was a pulse. No wonder he couldn't find them online.

I set my history homework aside and grabbed his computer.

He watched as I googled "popular media sites" and then clicked on a link to a website. Within seconds a list appeared with links to all the popular sites he had mangled.

"There you go, Dad," I said, handing his computer back to him.

"Thanks, Nikki!" He beamed. "I really appreciate your help. As a matter of fact, I'd like you to have these!"

He took out his wallet and handed me what I thought at first were dollar bills ☺! Only it wasn't money. It was gift cards ☹. Four "Big Bucks" gift cards to Queasy Cheesy pizza parlor, to be exact: "Good for one FREE pizza and large soda on Saturdays 1:00–3:00 p.m."

"Thanks, Dad." I smiled.

I had a hunch he might have gotten the gift cards from the owner after exterminating the place. But since I might actually be EATING there, I didn't want to know the dirty details.

I guess I could always sell the gift cards on the INTERWEB for some cold cash. Right, Dad?!

☺!!

SUNDAY, MAY 25—4:30 P.M.
IN MY BEDROOM

Today it was raining like crazy! Which meant I was trapped inside the house with my NUTTY family ☹!

I decided to spend some quality time lounging in bed, writing in my diary (about you-know-who!) while nibbling on chocolate.

So I brought out my secret stash of candy ☺!

I actually had to keep it hidden or Brianna would gobble up every last piece in less than sixty seconds.

Hey! I've seen her do it!

TWICE ☹!

I guess Mom wanted to take full advantage of the rainy day. So she decided we needed to have some Family Sharing Time.

"Now it's time for Board Game Madness!" she announced cheerfully as we finished lunch. . . .

MOM ANNOUNCES BOARD GAME MADNESS!

I guess no one was ready for "FUN, FUN, FUN!" because the room was suddenly so quiet, you could hear the rainwater gurgling into the sewer drains outside.

On second thought, that sound was Brianna greedily GUZZLING a glass of Princess Sugar Plum punch.

"I really wish I could join the fun, dear!" Dad exclaimed. "But the big championship game is about to come on!"

"Same here, Mom! I'd LOVE to play an exciting board game with you!" I lied. "But my FAVE reality show, *My Very Rich and Trashy Life!*, will be on soon, and it's the thrilling finale!"

As soon as Dad and I got up from the table to leave, Mom shot us her evil sit-your-butts-back-down-if-you-know-what's-good-for-you look.

So of course we quickly returned to our chairs and sat down.

It's NEVER a good idea to tick off Mom.

As the wise old saying goes, "If Mom's NOT happy, then NOBODY'S happy!"

Which is actually just the trendier "mommy power" version of the wise old saying "Misery LOVES company!"

"YAY! It's Board Game Madness!" Brianna cheered. "I'll go get a really FUN board game! Be right back!"

Mom escorted Dad and me into the family room like a seasoned prison guard.

I almost expected her to handcuff us to the couch to prevent us from attempting a dangerous felonious act like turning on the TV.

About five minutes later Brianna came skipping into the room with a small bag behind her back and an old pizza box covered in finger paint and glitter.

315

"Look at this! I made my OWN game! It's called Brianna's Funnest Game Ever! You're gonna LOVE it! Can we play it?! Can we, Mom? PLEEEEASE?" Brianna pleaded. . . .

BRIANNA'S FUNNEST GAME EVER!

"We'd LOVE to play your game, sweetheart!" Mom smiled. "It's going to be FUN!"

Brianna opened her pizza box.

Inside was a handmade game board with random squares and colorful crayon scribbles that made no sense WHATSOEVER!

I couldn't tell which direction to move or where the finish line was.

It looked like she'd just CHEWED up some crayons and SPIT them out on the paper. With her eyes closed.

"Okay! I'm gonna be the game boss," Brianna announced. "Daddy, you can be the paper clip, and Mommy, you can be the penny."

She handed them their game pieces.

"Cool! I get to be the cute Barbie shoe!" I smiled, picking up a tiny pink sparkly high heel.

"NUH-UH!" Brianna grunted, and snatched it right out of my hand. "That's MINE! Remember, it's MY game! I made it, so I'M the BOSS of it!"

Then she stuck her tongue out at me.

I folded my arms and glared at her.

"Then what am I supposed to use to play your game?! There's nothing left!" I grumbled.

Brianna checked inside the box, and sure enough, there WEREN'T any more game pieces.

But she just SHRUGGED her shoulders at me like it WASN'T her problem!

That's when I got a BRILLIANT idea! . . .

"OH NO! It looks like I won't be able play your game, Brianna! I'm SO disappointed!" I pretend-pouted, like I was about to cry. "I guess I'll just have to go watch the finale of My Very Rich and Trashy

Life! while you guys have all the FUN! But I'll get over it! BYE!"

"Hey! Wait a minute!" Brianna grinned as she peeled off a moldy piece of pepperoni that was stuck to the bottom of the box. "Here, Nikki! THIS is YOUR game piece!" . . .

EWWW!!

"I don't want that nasty thing!" I shrieked.

"But it's the BEST one!" Brianna exclaimed. "If you get hungry and want a snack, you can chew on it! Then, when it's your turn to move again, you just put the pepperoni back on the game board. I bet you can chew it for hours! Just like gum."

That's when I threw up in my mouth a little.

"MOM?!" I whined, waiting for her to intervene.

"Nikki, you're SPOILING the fun!" Mom lectured. "Brianna worked really hard on this game, so simmer down! Just take the pepperoni and try to be a good sport, okay?"

I begrudgingly picked up my NASTY pepperoni, trying to avoid the fuzzy mold, and dropped it on the "start" box, which was misspelled "stat."

"Mommy, you go first," Brianna said.

Mom rolled the die and moved four spaces.

"Now, this is the fun part!" Brianna squealed, and pulled out a stack of index cards written in black marker in her sloppy handwriting. "You have to do whatever the card says!"

However, instead of taking a card from the top of the stack, Brianna quickly sorted through them until she found one she liked.

"Here, Mommy. This is YOUR card!"

Mom read the card. . . .

> YOU ARE NICE AND PRETTY LIKE PRINCESS SUGAR PLUM. MOVE FORWARD ~~SEVN~~ SEVEN SPACES!

"How sweet!" Mom smiled and moved her penny seven spaces. "This game is FUN!"

"Okay, Daddy. Your turn!" Brianna chirped.

Dad rolled the die and moved five spaces.

Then Brianna selected a card. Dad read . . .

TODAY IS YOUR ~~LUCKY~~ Lucky DAY! DO THE "HOKEY POKEY" AND THEN MOVE AHEAD SIX SPACES!

"Woo-hoo!" Dad exclaimed. He hopped to his feet and did a rendition of the "Hokey Pokey" that included the chicken dance and some moves he stole from a Justin Bieber video.

Ugh!

Now I'll never be able to enjoy that video again without thinking of Dad's "Hokey Pokey"!

Next it was MY turn.

I tossed the die and moved three spaces.

"UH–OH!" Brianna said, reading the card she had selected for me.

She handed it to me, and I read it out loud. . . .

YOU ARE UGLY AND EAT BOOGERS!
YOU LOSE A TURN!
SORRY! ☹

"WHAT?!" I shouted. "That's NOT FAIR! Why do I have to be the ugly, booger-eating . . . LOSER?!"

"Because it's MY game and I make the RULES!" Brianna said, all snotty-like, with her hand on her hip.

"Okay, FINE!" I grumped. "I thought this was supposed to be FUN!"

I was SO over Brianna's STUPID game!

"Hey, everyone, NOW it's MY turn!" Brianna giggled. She rolled the die and moved her Barbie shoe three spaces.

"Now I get a card!" she said as she quickly sorted through the stack until she found one she liked.

"OH, GOODY! My card says . . ."

> YOU ARE THE BESTEST PLAYER AND GET TO HAVE THREE PIECES OF OF CANDY FROM THE JACKPOT CANDY STASH! CONGRATULATIONS!!!

"WHAT jackpot candy stash?!" I exclaimed.

"THIS ONE!" Brianna answered as she grabbed the plastic bag and opened it.

I almost had a . . .

HEART ATTACK!

Inside was my PRECIOUS candy stash!!!

THAT BRATTY LITTLE THIEF HAD SNUCK INTO MY ROOM AND STOLEN MY ENTIRE STASH OF CANDY?!!

"NO WAY!!" I protested. "I HATE this CRUDDY game. GIMME BACK MY CANDY, BRIANNA!"

"Aw, come on, Nikki! It's just candy. You can always get more!" Dad scolded me. "Let's just try to have fun playing your little sister's game!"

"I agree! This is an opportunity for you to be an excellent role model for Brianna. So try not to be a SORE LOSER!" Mom admonished me.

It's no wonder I had a really bad attitude about the whole thing.

Every time it was MY turn, I ended up with a stupid card that said something like . . .

> YoU GoTS CooTiES WiThouT
> A CooTiE SHoT!
> Go to JAiL!
> SORRY!!! 🙁

Or . . .

> YoU STiNKS REALLy BAd
> ANd ~~NEd~~ NEED A BATh!
> GO BACK to ~~STAT~~ STArt. ANd
> thEN LOSE A TURN!! SORRY!!!!! 🙁

And whenever it was Brianna's turn, she got to eat several more pieces of MY candy. I sat there GLARING at the three of them in complete DISGUST! I couldn't believe I was being FORCED by my very OWN parents to watch my bratty sister DEVOUR my candy during the finale of *My Very Rich and Trashy Life!*

I was very tempted to call the authorities and report them for CHILD ABUSE ☹!!

326

Finally Brianna had made an ingenious plan to get her GRUBBY little hands on my PROPERTY!

By the end of the game, my sister had eaten almost half of my candy! She had chocolate all over her face and hands and was looking a little queasy. . . .

"Goodness! I think this game has gotten completely out of hand!" Mom said, looking a bit flustered.

Dad scooped Brianna up off the floor. "You've had way too many sweets, young lady. I think you need to get some rest to cure that tummy ache."

"But I wanna keep playing!" she whined in a weak voice. "I NEVER get to EAT as much of Nikki's CANDY as I want!"

AHA!

Just as I had suspected!!

The whole point of Brianna's game was to get into my stash, and Mom and Dad had fallen for it.

I'll give Brianna points for being a pigtailed evil genius in pink My Little Pony sneakers!

But I refuse to feel all that sorry for her.

The next time we have Board Game Madness, we're going to play a RIGGED game MY way!

My board game will be called BROCCOLI-OPOLY, and it'll feature ALL the foods that Brianna HATES!!

Watch your back, little sister!

You're going to get a big green nasty PAYBACK! And it's going to be HEALTHY!

I can't wait to give Brianna a special card that says...

Today is your lucky day! You get to drink a gallon of green smoothie! Sorry! ☹

And who knows! If I'm feeling really VENGEFUL, I just might toss in some MOLDY PEPPERONI for extra flavor!

Anyway, since *My Very Rich and Trashy Life!* is over, I might as well try to finish the homework I've been procrastinating all weekend.

I'm actually looking forward to school tomorrow.

I'll finally get to meet the NHH exchange student, Andrea.

It's going to be FUN!

SQUEEEEEE!!

☺!!

MONDAY, MAY 26—12:15 P.M.
IN THE GIRLS' BATHROOM

I was supposed to hang out with Chloe, Zoey, and Brandon during lunch to help them with their projects.

Chloe and Zoey want to start shooting practice videos next week.

And Brandon needs to get the Fuzzy Friends donation page up and running before their annual charity drive, which starts on June 5.

But, unfortunately, I had to cancel because I have an earlier lunch and I had to meet the exchange student at noon. And since this student ambassador thing is MANDATORY, I didn't have a choice.

At noon I grabbed my welcome sign and rushed down to the office.

I waited right outside the door. . . .

WELCOME,
ANDREA,
TO WCD!!

But soon it became very clear that I'd made a
HUGE mistake. HOW could I have accidentally gotten
something as simple as a NAME wrong?!

The exchange student's name WASN'T Andrea! . . .

... HIS NAME WAS ANDRÉ!

I just stared at him in shock, with my mouth hanging open, and blurted out . . .

"OMG! You're a GUY?!"

Of course, after I said that, I felt REALLY STUPID.

I could feel my face flush with embarrassment.

He gave me a big smile and nodded.

"Yes, Nikki. I'm a guy. I'm sorry if you're a little disappointed."

"NO! I'm n—not!" I stammered. "It would be STUPID to feel that way just because you're a guy! Uh, I mean . . . for ME. I'm NOT calling YOU stupid if YOU feel that way. Because most guys are—I mean, AREN'T! What I'm really trying to say is, um, is it ME or is it really WARM in here?"

Suddenly André leaned in closer and stared at my welcome sign. . . .

ANDRÉ NOTICES MY SIGN.

I tried to cover up the misspelled name and act like it wasn't a big deal. . . .

But inside I was totally FREAKING OUT!

OMG! I could NOT believe I had told a GUY all that VERY personal stuff about my hairy legs, my crush, and "Branikki."

WHAT if he tells the ENTIRE school ☹?! Worse yet, WHAT if he tells MY entire school and HIS entire school ☹?!! My reputation would be more PATHETIC than it already is. The gossip could follow me into high school and totally ruin the best years of my life.

Suddenly I realized that André was staring at me.

"Um . . . are you okay?" he asked.

I plastered a fake smile across my face and very cheerfully said, "André, it's nice to finally meet you. I hope you enjoy your week here at Westchester Country Day Middle School. Are you ready for your tour?"

This is what I learned about him. André's dad is French and works for the United Nations, and his mom is an American journalist. His mom and stepdad live here, and his dad has a home both here and in

Paris. He said he studied at the Louvre museum's program for gifted students and would LOVE to show me around the city if I ever visited Paris.

Then the WEIRDEST thing happened. André kind of stared at me and asked if he could call me Nicole instead of Nikki. He said the name Nicole is popular in France and is a beautiful and intriguing name, meaning "victorious," that fits me so much better.

OMG! I almost DIED from the massive drop in blood pressure due to intense blushing.

"Um . . . sure, André! Actually, my real name IS Nicole," I gushed, and then giggled.

André seems almost . . . PERFECT! Like, straight out of one of Chloe's teen romance books perfect!

I don't know what's WRONG with me. When he asked me what my favorite subject is, I completely blanked.

I also couldn't remember my locker combo.

I was looking for my phone to type in his cell number when I had it in my hand.

That's when I very politely asked André to wait in the library (I found the library ONLY because we were standing right in front of it) while I went to the girls' bathroom across the hall to check to see if I had left my BRAIN in there!

Yes! I just said my BRAIN! Or maybe I accidentally flushed it down the toilet when I was in there earlier today. Because right now I'm CLEARLY functioning WITHOUT ONE ☹!!

So I rushed to the girls' bathroom to try to pull myself together, because I was having a MASSIVE MELTDOWN! I gave myself a pep talk: Just stay calm. YOU can do this. Breathe deeply and repeat . . .

"I CAN DO THIS! I CAN DO THIS! I CAN DO THIS! I CAN DO THIS!"

Great job! Now just look at yourself in the mirror and say it one last time. . . .

ME, HAVING A MASSIVE MELTDOWN!!

To make matters WORSE, I just got a really important e-mail.

But I'm afraid to open and read it.

I'm feeling SUPERnervous and totally stressed out! But mostly I feel . . . OVERWHELMED!!

So I desperately texted Chloe and Zoey a message:

NIKKI: HEEEEEEEEEEEEELP ☹!! I've completely lost my mind! And since it's the only one I have, I'm leaving to go search for it. But if my mind happens to wander back here before I find it, please do me a really big favor and lock it in the janitor's closet until I return.

ZOEY: ??????????

CHLOE: R U insane?!!!!!

NIKKI: Probably. Just left a ridiculously cute guy in the library and rushed to the bathroom to SCREAM at myself in the mirror! Be right back! Checking toilet for my missing brain.

CHLOE: ????????

ZOEY: ????????

NOTE TO SELF!!

Do not open the e-mail you just received from
Madame Danielle, the French teacher from NHH,
with the subject line "RE: DECISION REGARDING
ARTS & CULTURE STUDENT TRIP TO PARIS."

WHY?

Because if I have to deal with any more DRAMA,
my HEAD is going to EXPLODE!!

And I do NOT want to be publicly HUMILIATED
when my head EXPLODES at school in front of
the entire student body.

And, um . . . André.

☹!!

MONDAY—2:30 P.M.
AT MY LOCKER

I've spent almost two hours giving André a complete tour of WCD.

Unlike some NHH students, he seems pretty friendly and has a wicked sense of humor.

We got along really well, and get this! WE BOTH LOVE ART!

The only problem is that he makes me SUPERnervous!

I don't know why. He just . . . DOES!!

André hasn't had a chance to meet any other students yet.

Although, after my crazy text messages, Chloe and Zoey are DYING to meet HIM.

In just the past hour my BFFs have texted me more than a dozen times.

My phone was chiming so much I turned off
the sound.

I couldn't believe they were actually begging me to
take a selfie with André and SEND it to them so
they could "see what a HUNK he is!"

Sorry, Chloe and Zoey ☹! But I've only known the
guy for, like, five minutes.

I am NOT going to embarrass myself by saying,
"Um, André, would you mind taking a quick selfie
with me? My BFFs are just DYING to see how
HUNKY you are!"

Like, how JUVENILE would that be?!

At least Chloe and Zoey weren't too upset with me
earlier when I told them I couldn't meet them today
to work on their video project.

After André and I completed the tour, I showed
him his locker and told him to text me if he had
questions about anything.

He had to leave school early for a dentist appointment, so I walked him to the main entrance.

I thought his dad was waiting to pick him up at the front of the school, but he said it was his chauffeur! . . .

Yes! The guy is in middle school and has his own CHAUFFEUR!

Can you believe it?!

Must be NICE!!

We agreed to meet tomorrow morning at my locker and then head off to class.

After André left, I decided to go ahead and read that e-mail about the Paris trip in August. I wasn't supposed to find out if I'd been accepted for another week still, but I was pretty sure this was a big fat REJECTION!

Even if my head exploded, the only person around was MacKenzie, and she couldn't care less.

Unless, of course, a teeny tiny bit splattered on her shoe. In which case, she'd have a complete meltdown!

I held my breath as I nervously read the e-mail: "Dear Nikki, Blah, blah, blah-blah, blah-blah . . ."

ME, NERVOUSLY READING THE E-MAIL

I ACTUALLY GOT A SPOT ON THE TRIP!!

Unfortunately, I didn't get a chance to read the ENTIRE e-mail because I was very RUDELY interrupted.

By guess who?! . . .

MacKenzie ☹!!

"So, it must be a family business trip? I didn't know Paris had a ROACH problem!" she giggled.

Okay, yeah. My dad owns a bug extermination business. Big hairy deal!

But why did girlfriend have to start tossing NASTY insults?

I wasn't even TALKING to her ☹!

That's when I suddenly stared at MacKenzie in horror.

"OMG!! MACKENZIE!! IT'S YOUR . . . NOSE!!" I gasped. "I can't believe it. Your NOSE!"

She immediately panicked and touched her nose.

"WHAT'S WRONG WITH MY NOSE?!"

"IT'S IN MY BUSINESS! AGAIN!" I exclaimed. "PLEASE! KEEP YOUR NOSE OUT OF MY BUSINESS!"

MacKenzie just rolled her eyes at me. "Nikki, instead of worrying about my nose, you should worry about your face. You're so BUTT UGLY that when dogs first meet you, they sniff your FACE! I know you're JEALOUS, Nikki, but don't HATE ME because I'm beautiful!"

"You actually think I'm jealous?! MacKenzie, you have FAKE hair, FAKE nails, FAKE eyelashes, and a FAKE tan! I can actually BUY your beauty SUPERcheap at the Dollar Store!"

"Well, don't feel TOO bad, Nikki! You can always PHOTOSHOP the photos of your face!"

"At least I have hope, MacKenzie. You can't Photoshop your BUTT-UGLY PERSONALITY! But your dad's really rich! So you can ask him to BUY you a new one for your birthday!"

That's when MacKenzie just totally ignored me.

She glanced in her mirror and slathered on, like, four layers of Pretty Peach sparkly lip gloss.

Then she flipped her hair, rolled her eyes at me one final time, and SASHAYED AWAY.

I just HATE it when MacKenzie SASHAYS!

MacKenzie is SOOO aggravating!

She makes me want to . . .

SCREAM!!

But instead of thinking about MacKenzie, I decided to concentrate on my FABULOUS summer plans!

They were EXCITING enough to make even MacKenzie GREEN with envy!

JUNE: Um . . . have I mentioned yet that my birthday is in June?

JULY: I'll be on tour with my BFFs in July.

AUGUST: I'll do Paris in August.

SEPTEMBER: And then high school in September!

I was NOT about to let MacKenzie's silly MEAN GIRL shenanigans RUIN my good mood!

Besides, I was too distracted. I was already envisioning myself taking selfies in PARIS! . . .

ME IN PARIS

This is going to be the BEST summer of my
ENTIRE life!! 😊!!

OMG! I finally just read that ENTIRE e-mail ☹!

And now I have a REALLY big problem!

Actually, BIG does NOT even begin to describe it. It's . . .

HUMONGOUS!

This is my problem. . . .

I WAS AWARDED THE TRIP TO PARIS ☹!!

I know. This SHOULD be really GOOD news.

I should be doing my Snoopy "happy dance" on top of my bed, NOT lying here SUPERdepressed, staring at the wall and SULKING.

I reread the e-mail that I'd received from Madame Danielle for the FIFTH time. . . .

FROM: Madame Danielle

TO: Nikki Maxwell

RE: Decision Regarding Arts & Culture Student Trip to Paris

Dear Nikki,

Congratulations! You have been selected to participate in the Arts & Culture Student Trip to Paris, France, sponsored this year by North Hampton Hills International Academy.

You will be receiving your Paris Student Travel Registration Packet very soon. However, please be aware that the attached Parental Permission Form must be signed and returned by the deadline of Wednesday, June 11, to reserve your spot in the program.

We are happy to announce that we are expanding our program from ten to fourteen days. To accommodate this change, our trip will take place this year from July 7 to July 20. If you have any questions or concerns, please feel free to contact me.

Best regards,
Madame Danielle

I was hoping that I had somehow simply misread the dates of the trip.

But I hadn't!

My trip to Paris is scheduled for two weeks in July, right smack in the middle of my BAD BOYZ tour!

NOOOOOOO ☹!!

That was me SCREAMING.

I can't believe I'm going to have to choose between the two—PARIS or the CONCERT TOUR ☹! It's going to be almost IMPOSSIBLE to do!

The fourteen-day trip to Paris is a once-in-a-lifetime opportunity for me to study art at the world-famous Louvre.

However, the Bad Boyz tour will be an awesome experience for my friends and me! And I'm sure it would increase the popularity of our band.

I think I need to talk to Brandon, Chloe, and Zoey about this since it involves them.

But I'm pretty sure they'll probably just tell me to follow my heart.

I think they'll support whatever decision I make.

I'm so LUCKY to have friends like them!

OMG!

This is the most difficult decision I've ever had to make in my entire life.

☹!!

My day with André has been a complete CIRCUS!

When I introduced him to Chloe and Zoey this morning, they pretty much lost their minds.

"André, these are my BFFs, Chloe Garcia and Zoey Franklin," I said.

"Hi, Chloe and Zoey, it's nice to meet you!" André said as he shook their hands. "Any BFF of Nicole's is a BFF of mine!"

"Hi, André!" Chloe said, batting her eyes really fast like her contacts had completely dried out or something.

"Nice to meet you, André!" Zoey practically whispered, and then giggled uncontrollably.

I didn't know what had gotten into my friends. WHY were they acting so silly?!

358

"So, André, are you ready to head off to our first class?" I asked.

"I'll come too, if you don't mind," Chloe giggled.

"Me too!" Zoey squealed.

That's when I noticed that a small crowd of girls, including MacKenzie, had gathered. They were giggling and staring at André.

MacKenzie gave André a big smile and waved. "Hi, I'm MacKenzie Hollister! Welcome to WCD. If you need anything at all, including a SMART, cute, and fashionable friend to hang out with, just let ME know!"

Well, at least she was right about the cute and fashionable part.

I could not believe it when she started twirling her hair around and around, trying to secretly hypnotize him into doing her EVIL bidding (she had tried that same stunt with Brandon!). . . .

MACKENZIE, FLIRTING WITH ANDRÉ

Everywhere we went, girls stopped, stared, giggled, and whispered.

I guess you could say that André was a VERY popular guy at my school.

It was SO embarrassing!

I actually apologized for some of their more juvenile behavior.

But André just smiled and shrugged it off. "No problem, Nicole. Today I'm the new kid. But by tomorrow they'll all be IGNORING me like they do at North Hampton Hills," he joked.

Unfortunately, things got a little tense in bio.

In all my classes, the teachers had allowed André to sit next to me since he was a visiting student.

But when Brandon saw André sitting in HIS seat, he just kind of stood there staring at him with this look that I'd never seen before. . . .

BRANDON MEETS ANDRÉ.

Brandon looked at me and then André, back to me and then André, and finally back to me, like . . .

NIKKI, **WHO** IS THIS GUY AND **WHY** IS HE SITTING IN **MY** SEAT?!!

Finally the teacher cleared her throat. "Mr. Roberts, since André will be our guest student this week, could you please politely find another seat?"

"Um . . . sure!" Brandon shrugged as he slid into the only empty seat. "Hey, bro, welcome to WCD," he kind of muttered.

For some reason I felt bad for Brandon. The whole scene was just kind of . . . **AWKWARD!!**

That's when it occurred to me that although I had mentioned the student ambassador thing with André to Chloe and Zoey, I had completely forgotten to tell Brandon the reason I'd canceled meeting him earlier.

No wonder he was a little confused. And very highly ANNOYED. . . .

363

MACKENZIE

BRANDON, KIND OF TICKED OFF ABOUT
THE NEW SEATING ARRANGEMENT!

Not only had Brandon lost HIS seat to some dude in a uniform from NHH, but now he was STUCK sitting next to bubble brain MacKenzie.

For the rest of the week!

I sighed and bit my lip.

JUST GREAT ☹!!

André has been at our school less than a day, and Chloe and Zoey have turned into giggling puddles of drool and Brandon was so irritated I could almost see the smoke coming out of his ears.

I have a feeling it's going to be a . . .

VERY.

LONG.

WEEK!

☹!!

WEDNESDAY, MAY 28—10:50 A.M.
AT MY LOCKER

André and I get along really well, and he's fitting right in at WCD.

Most of the students seem to really LOVE him!

And by "most students," I mean . . . GIRLS.

Some of the guys seem really bent out of shape with all the attention he's been getting.

"What's up with the dude in the cheesy school uniform?!" I overheard a few jocks complain yesterday when a dozen girls lined up to take selfies with André like he was a celeb or something.

Personally, I think those guys are a little jelly (a.k.a. jealous) of André.

At least Brandon is being a good sport about the whole thing.

He told me not to worry about trying to help out with the Fuzzy Friends website since I'm going to be SUPERbusy with my student ambassador duties.

Brandon is such a SWEETHEART ☺!

(Although he did text me this morning that he can hardly wait for André to go back to Hogwarts so he can get his seat back in bio.)

I just hope Brandon is able to get everything done in time for the annual fund-raiser since they need all the money they can get to keep the animal rescue center open.

Chloe and Zoey are my BFFs and I love them, but they've been acting so silly and immature around André that it's an EMBARRASSMENT!

The whole selfie FIASCO yesterday was actually THEIR fault. They practically BEGGED André for a selfie, and to be nice he agreed.

So the four of us took one together. . . .

ANDRÉ TAKES A SELFIE WITH
CHLOE, ZOEY, AND ME.

MacKenzie was at her locker the entire time,
pretending like my BFFs and I didn't EXIST.

So of course SHE asked André for a selfie too.

After that it was two girls from the drama club and then the ENTIRE cheerleading squad!

Pretty soon there were a dozen girls in line, all waiting to take a selfie with André.

But here's the really WEIRD part! . . .

EVERYONE kept telling me what a CUTE COUPLE André and I were.

I was like, "Um . . . NO WAY! We're actually just FRIENDS. We're only hanging out because I'm a student ambassador and it's MANDATORY."

But they just smiled like I was LYING to them and started WHISPERING to each other.

Of course I wondered what was going on!

So to avoid all the DRAMA that had occurred yesterday, I texted André and asked him to meet me in the library. I figured we'd hang out there for a while and then go straight to class.

I was surprised when he showed up with a bag from the CupCakery. . . .

ANDRÉ, BRINGING BREAKFAST

He'd purchased orange juice and extra-large cinnamon buns with cream cheese frosting. The best part was that they were still warm!

Since I'd skipped breakfast to get to school on time, my stomach was making loud grinding noises like a busted garbage disposal.

OMG! Everything was DELISH!

"So, do you have any exciting plans for the summer?" André asked.

JUST GREAT ☹!! The last thing I wanted to talk about was my summer scheduling DISASTER!

He must have seen a look of pure anguish flash across my face or something. Because even after I shrugged and muttered, "Not really," he stopped eating and just stared at me.

"Really?! Are your parents shipping you off to boot camp or something?" he teased.

Instead of answering, I just took a big bite of my cinnamon bun and chewed, trying not to look as annoyed as I felt. I'd already blabbed WAAAY too much about my PATHETIC life in those e-mails I'd sent André.

Hey, I barely even KNOW the guy!

"I WISH they were shipping me off to camp!" I finally sighed. "Then I wouldn't feel so guilty for being selfish and totally ruining my BFFs' plans for the summer!"

"Nicole, you don't seem to me like the type of person who'd purposely hurt your friends."

"Listen, André, it's REALLY complicated, and we don't have that much time," I muttered.

He glanced at his watch. "Actually, we have two minutes and fifteen seconds. I suggest you talk really, really fast!" He smiled.

So I reluctantly told him EVERYTHING! . . .

ANYWAY, I'M CONFUSED! I CAN'T DECIDE IF I SHOULD GO TO PARIS OR ON TOUR WITH MY BAND!

WOW, NICOLE! THAT'S A REALLY GOOD PROBLEM TO HAVE!

I SPILL MY GUTS TO ANDRÉ!

"Seriously, André! It's a BIG problem for ME if I disappoint my friends. I really care about them!" I explained.

"Wait a minute!" he exclaimed. "Let me get this straight. YOU have an all-expenses-paid trip for two weeks in Paris to study at the Louvre, and you're worried about your friends being MAD at you?! Really?! Sorry, Nicole, but you need some NEW friends!"

"Well, I don't know for SURE that they'd be mad at me. But I'd be mad at MYSELF. I'd basically be ditching my BFFs and the Bad Boyz tour that we've been planning together for MONTHS! Like, WHO does that?! Only the WORST friend EVER!" I grumbled.

"I'll be perfectly honest with you. I'd LOVE for you to come to Paris, Nicole! We'd have a great time hanging out together, and I could show you around the city. But that's a decision only YOU can make."

"OMG! Studying art in Paris would be a dream come true. Everyone was really HAPPY for me a few weeks ago when I first told them about it. I guess I need to sit down with them and explain that both events are scheduled at the same time. And if I go to Paris,

374

I WON'T be able to go with them on the Bad Boyz tour. I just hope they won't be too disappointed!"

Anyway, after hashing everything out with André, I decided to do the mature and responsible thing.

I sent Chloe, Zoey, and Brandon a text asking them to meet me after school in the library to discuss some really important news.

André said I shouldn't worry because everything was going to work out fine. I was so grateful for his help and advice that I told him I'd give him one of the Queasy Cheesy gift cards from my dad.

I just hope he's right!

☺!

AAAAAAHHH ☹!!

Okay. THAT was me SCREAMING!!

WHY?

Because I am having yet another MELTDOWN!!

YES, I know! It's the SECOND one this week, and it's only Wednesday!

This is what happened. . . .

Chloe, Zoey, and Brandon were excited to meet me in the library after school.

André and I have been attending classes together for ONLY two DAYS, but my friends were acting more like it had been two WEEKS.

"Nikki, we know your student ambassador duties are mandatory, but we really miss hanging out with you!" Zoey complained.

"I totally agree!" Chloe grumbled. "André is a nice and cute guy, but it kind of feels like he has KIDNAPPED our BFF!"

"Yeah! Someone needs to tell that dude this place is a middle school, NOT a DAY CARE CENTER!" Brandon griped. "Personally, Nikki, I think he's into you."

"No way! It's NOT like that at all," I protested. "Come on, guys. Be NICE!"

But deep down I was surprised and very flattered that Brandon was acting a little jealous. Maybe it meant Brandon REALLY liked me.

Although, to be honest, it had never occurred to me that a guy like André would be interested in a nice and dorky girl like . . . ME!

I mean, he could totally date one of those gorgeous teen Disney starlets.

Hey, I'd be lucky to have ONE guy interested in me.

But TWO guys?!

OMG!

That sounds like something straight out of a fairy tale. . . .

Once upon a time, Princess Nikki was standing on her balcony gazing at her beautiful kingdom.

Suddenly the handsome Prince Brandon appeared and said, "Princess Nikki, would you like to go for a walk with ME in the meadow?"

But before she could answer, the handsome Prince André appeared and said, "Princess Nicole, would you like to walk with ME in the meadow?!"

Then they dueled over her with swords. . . .

BRANDON AND ANDRÉ DUEL OVER ME
WITH SWORDS!

Zoey interrupted my daydream. "So, what's the important news? We're DYING to know!"

"Is it a SURPRISE?!" Chloe squealed. "I LOVE surprises!"

"Well, actually, it has to do with the Bad Boyz tour this summer," I answered hesitantly.

"I'm ready to ROCK!" Zoey exclaimed. "My family will be going on a two-week vacation to Maui without me. I decided our tour was more important!"

"Really?!" I muttered.

"Yeah, me too!" Chloe said. "I FINALLY landed us tickets to Comic-Con in San Diego. But I gave them away since we're going to be on tour that week!"

"You DID?!" I groaned.

"Same here!" Brandon said. "I've been on a waiting list for a photography camp, and I found out last week that I got in! But I've already given up my spot since we'll be on tour in July."

"You DIDN'T!" I moaned.

All three of my friends stared at me eagerly as they waited for me to share my VERY important news.

Suddenly I felt really . . . GUILTY! Each of my friends had made a personal sacrifice to go on that tour.

"Well, actually, it's REALLY hard for me to find the right words," I muttered.

"Come on, Nikki! You can tell us ANYTHING!" Zoey said encouragingly.

I took a deep breath and closed my eyes.

"Okay! Chloe, Zoey, and Brandon, I realize we've been planning this Bad Boyz tour for MONTHS! But I really need to let you know that . . . I CAN'T—"

That's when my BFFs very enthusiastically and very rudely interrupted me. . . .

MY SUPERENTHUSIASTIC BFFS

Then Chloe, Zoey, and Brandon started cheering! And WOO-HOOing! And high-fiving each other!

They were acting like they had just won the Super Bowl or something.

Somehow we'd had a MAJOR miscommunication about the Bad Boyz tour.

"Nikki, we realize our show is a huge responsibility for you," Zoey said supportively.

"But always remember! WE'RE in this thing TOGETHER!" Chloe said, giving me jazz hands.

"Yeah! WE GOT THIS!" Brandon exclaimed.

Then the three of them gave me a big hug!

The massive outpouring of love, support, and enthusiasm from my friends was SO touching that I got a HUGE lump in my throat.

I knew I was going to have to tell my friends the

TRUTH sooner or later. But right then I was kind of leaning more toward . . .

LATER ☹!

As much as I wanted to wait, though, I knew I had to get it over with. Since it seemed almost impossible for me to TELL them the bad news, I thought it might be easier if I just SHOWED them.

"Listen, guys, I want you to read an e-mail that I received on Monday. That will pretty much explain everything," I said.

I pulled up my e-mails to show them the one I'd gotten about the trip to Paris.

But that's when I noticed a brand-new e-mail from a popular social media website saying that a post I was tagged in had received more than twenty-five comments and likes.

It said "Cute pic of André and Nikki!" I opened the e-mail and just stared at the photo in shock. . . .

ME, FREAKING OUT OVER
A PIC OF ME ONLINE!

It FINALLY made sense why everyone was GOSSIPING
yesterday about André and me being a couple.

Someone had taken a photo of André and me at school.

But the sign I was holding had been altered. . . .

Nikki & André hang out at WCD! Too CUTE!

SelfieChic: ADORABLENESS!

LuvMyLipGloss: I heard they met while she was visiting NHH. Maybe LOVE at first sight?!

Flawless: They are perfect together. I totally ship them!

CheerGirl: CUTEST couple EVER!

LuvMyLipGloss: Hanging out with him is definitely an upgrade from her two dorky BFFs.

Diva124: What about poor Brandon?

SelfieChic: Looks like he'll have to get over it.

Diva124: I'll take him ☺!

How could people talk about my friends like that?!

I couldn't bear to read another comment! Whoever posted that pic is obviously just trying to stir up DRAMA, because my REAL sign said "Welcome, Andrea, to WCD!!"

NOT "I missed you, André!!"

I sighed in frustration and clicked off that website.

That's when I realized my friends were STILL eagerly waiting for me to show them the e-mail I had mentioned.

"So, what do you need to show us?" Zoey asked. "Is it an e-mail from Trevor Chase?"

"OMG! It's an e-mail from the BAD BOYZ! RIGHT?!" Chloe shouted hysterically. "If it is, I think I'm going to DIE!"

JUST GREAT ☹!

Even my e-mail idea had turned into a HOT MESS!

"Listen, guys! I'm really sorry, but something just came up. I really need to GO! Right now! We can talk about this later, okay?" I said, trying to stay calm.

"Is something wrong, Nikki?!" Brandon asked, concerned.

"Um . . . NO! I just got an e-mail here . . . from my, um . . . MOM! And I have to go home to, uh . . .

babysit Brianna. Bye, guys!" I said as I quickly headed for the door.

"WHAT?!" Chloe and Zoey blinked in confusion.

"Wait a minute! Nikki, come back! Are you sure you're—" I didn't hear the rest of Brandon's question because I practically ran down the hall.

I had to get out of there before I burst into tears!

Right now I'm writing in my diary, trying to figure out how to fix this

DISASTER!

I'm pretty sure Chloe, Zoey, and Brandon hadn't seen that post yet.

If they had, I'm VERY sure they would have been upset enough to have mentioned it.

If/when Brandon finds out, I just hope he doesn't believe all the crazy gossip.

It might make him feel a little insecure (and extremely cruddy!) to hear rumors that André and I are a couple.

I already feel HORRIBLE for him!

And NOW I have to tell my BFFs about the trip to Paris AND the gossip about them online.

OH NO ☹! Daisy stole my peanut butter sandwich and got peanut butter EVERYWHERE! I actually had to change my clothes!

JUST GREAT ☹!! Now someone's ringing the doorbell.

OMG! I can't believe who's actually here!

It's . . .

BRANDON?!

☹!!

WEDNESDAY—7:00 P.M.
AT HOME

Brandon was at my front door! My first reaction was . . .

NOOOOO ☹!!

I was pretty sure he'd seen the photo online and had rushed over to my house to ask me about it.

I now had the perfect opportunity to be a mature and responsible adult and tell Brandon the TRUTH about EVERYTHING!

Like . . .

André and I are MERELY friends.

I met him for the first time in my life less than seventy-two hours ago.

I'm planning to ditch you, my BFFs, and the national Bad Boyz tour to hang out with him in Paris for two weeks!

Just ignore any photos you see of André and me.

And definitely don't believe any of the gossip.

Unfortunately, all of that sounded like a bunch of LIES. . . .

Even to ME ☹!

And I KNOW the truth!

So how could I expect Brandon to believe me?!!

The reality was that he probably wouldn't!

I didn't have a choice but to try to convince him.

I opened the door, grabbed Brandon's shoulders, and stared desperately into his eyes.

"Listen, Brandon! I know why you're here, and I don't blame you for being upset. But André and I are JUST friends! Nothing more! You gotta believe me!"

He just stared back at me, slightly surprised and totally confused. . . .

BRANDON STARES AT ME,
TOTALLY CONFUSED!

"Um . . . okay, Nikki. I think I understand. Does this mean that André is going to help out with Daisy's training session? Because today she's supposed to learn the sit and stay commands."

"OMG! It's Wednesday, and we have Daisy's training TODAY! So th—that's why you're here?!" I stammered.

"Um . . . is now a bad time?" Brandon asked.

"WHAT?! I mean . . . of COURSE not! I was just a little confused, that's all!" I babbled like an idiot. "Daisy is in the backyard."

"So what was all that stuff about André?" Brandon asked.

"Never mind! I'll grab us something to drink and meet you out back in a few minutes, okay?"

I could hardly believe Brandon was here for Daisy's second doggie obedience lesson!

NOT to grill me about my relationship with André and tell me what a hopelessly PATHETIC friend I am.

I actually felt totally RELIEVED!

Hey, why RUIN a fun evening hanging out with my crush?

So I decided NOT to bring up the trip to Paris, the Bad Boyz tour, or the online gossip.

Until . . .

LATER!

Since it was a warm evening, I made a delicious pitcher of ice-cold lemonade.

What better way for Brandon and me to CHILLAX than with a cool, refreshing drink!

I was carrying the tray of lemonade over to Brandon when I encountered a series of unfortunate events. . . .

Thanks to Daisy, Brandon and I had a very cold and refreshing lemonade SHOWER!

WE never got a chance to drink my lemonade.

But Daisy tasted it.

And she LOVED it!

After we'd finished with Daisy's lesson, I decided it was time to finally break the bad news.

"Listen, Brandon! I appreciate everything you've done for Daisy, but I really need to tell you—"

"Nikki, you DON'T have to THANK ME again!" Brandon smiled. Then he brushed his shaggy bangs out of his eyes and smiled at me all shy-like. "I really enjoy hanging out with you. As a matter of fact, I was wondering if you, um . . . wanted to go out to Queasy Cheesy for pizza this weekend?"

"Sure, Brandon! Of course. It would be fun," I answered very calmly.

But deep down inside I was elated and doing my Snoopy "happy dance." . . .

SQUEEEEEEE ☺!!

I'M SO HAPPY!!

I'M SO HAPPY!!

BRANDON ASKED ME TO HANG OUT AT QUEASY CHEESY!

We decided to text each other Saturday morning to arrange everything.

I know it's NOT actually a REAL date!

Since we're NOT actually a REAL couple!

YET!

But . . .

STILL☺!!

It's like really, really, really CLOSE to all of that without ACTUALLY being it.

So I decided NOT to RUIN the moment by bringing up other stuff.

Hey, when life gives you lemons, make lemonade!

Just try not to SPILL it all over your CRUSH!

I'm really lucky to have a friend like Brandon!

SQUEEEEEEEE!!

☺!!

This whole day has been one giant emotional
ROLLER COASTER ☹!

Another photo was posted online about an hour ago.
It was more gossip about André and me. . . .

Nikki & André ditch school to hang out?!

SelfieChic: Isn't this against the rules?!

LuvMyLipGloss: ONLY if they get caught ☺!

Diva124: Then they can do after-school detention TOGETHER! How romantic!

CheerGirl: Where'd they go?

Flawless: Maybe to the CupCakery? In Paris! On his family's private jet!

SelfieChic: I'm so JELLY!

LuvMyLipGloss: Poor André was probably trying to get away from her tacky, annoying BFFs, Chloe and Zoey!

OMG!

I was FURIOUS!

André and I did NOT ditch school together! He had simply left early for a dentist appointment.

I wonder who's posting this GARBAGE?!

Judging from the usernames, I can make a pretty good guess.

LuvMyLipGloss is probably MacKenzie, and SelfieChic is probably Tiffany from NHH.

I have no idea WHY they would do this to me.

Well, other than the fact that they both HATE my GUTS!!

The HUMILIATING part is that most of the students from WCD and NHH will probably read this stuff and believe it's TRUE!

It just occurred to me that posts like this are considered cyberbullying.

And both schools, WCD and NHH, have very strict rules against it.

Sometimes in life you have to do the right thing, even when it's difficult or unpopular.

Which means I need to PONDER a very COMPLEX and DIFFICULT question. . . .

WHY IS MY LIFE SUCH A GIANT BUCKET OF PUKE?!!

☹!!

I just got out of bed thirty minutes ago, but I'm STILL totally EXHAUSTED, mostly due to excessive WORRY and SLEEP deprivation ☹!

My life would be PERFECT if I could sleep late, watch cartoons, chillax, eat yummy snacks, take a nap, AND go to school for only HALF a day.

Yes, I'll admit it. I WISH I was back in kindergarten! My life was SO simple then.

I checked my e-mail and there weren't any new posts about André and me. Thank goodness!

I DID receive that packet of info about the Paris trip. It said the flight is going to be seven and a half hours, which is really long.

But it's going to be a BREEZE compared to the HORRIFIC ninety-minute plane trip I took with Brianna last summer when we went to visit my aunt in Indiana.

407

It started with a really long wait in line to get through airport security to board the plane. Which meant wandering through a crowded maze, taking off our shoes, and then walking into that thing that looks like a space pod.

Brianna was bored out of her mind and sticking a wad of bubble gum up her nose (I am NOT lying!), when she suddenly pointed and screamed, "HEY, LOOK!! A PUPPY!"

Sure enough, there was a security guy with a German shepherd on a leash sniffing for drugs, bombs, or dangerous toiletries—whatever those dogs are trained to sniff for.

"Brianna, that dog is busy working," my dad explained. "So please don't bother it, honey."

In spite of my dad's warning, she quickly DOVE under the divider, rushed over to the dog, threw her arms around it, and gave it a big hug.

My mom gasped and I frantically dashed after Brianna.

Luckily, the dog just sniffed her and licked her. . . .

409

The grumpy security guy scowled at Brianna and said, "Step AWAY from the dog, miss!"

Brianna's eyes got huge. My parents froze. I quickly grabbed Brianna's hand.

"Sorry, sir! She's just a little kid," I apologized.

But he just glared at us. "BOTH OF YOU! STEP AWAY FROM THE DOG!" he shouted.

Brianna and I scrambled back to our spot in line while the dog just wagged his tail.

My bratty little sister had almost gotten us arrested by attack-hugging a security dog, and we hadn't even made it to the plane yet.

Unfortunately, it went totally downhill from there.

Since we had left the house at 6:00 a.m., I was hoping she would sleep on the plane, but I couldn't have been more wrong!

She was so hyped up on sugar from an overpriced airport breakfast of doughnuts and hot chocolate that she probably wasn't going to sleep for at least a week. (Thanks a lot, MOM ☹!)

To make matters worse, this was Brianna's very first trip on a plane.

And, unfortunately, we didn't have four seats all together in the same row, because each row had only three seats.

My parents sat together, and I was stuck sitting with Brianna a few rows behind them.

Brianna demanded the window seat. So I was trapped between her and this businessman who kept on elbowing me as he typed on his laptop.

"Why aren't we flying?" she asked two seconds after we sat down.

"Brianna, people are still boarding the plane," I explained. "We'll be leaving soon, okay?!"

"How about now? Is it time yet? When are we going to flyyyyyyy??!!" she complained.

Mr. Laptop Guy was straight up trying to kill us WITH HIS EYES.

I mean, I wanted Brianna to shut up too! But why was he giving ME the EVIL EYE?!

Once everyone was seated, the flight attendant started her speech about what to do when the plane CRASHES into the OCEAN.

I'm not going to lie! That speech always makes me a little nervous. So I kind of understood when Brianna started to freak out.

But my little sister took FREAKING OUT to a whole new level!

"Is my seat belt tight enough? Promise you'll do my air mask first, Nikki! A WATER landing?! WHERE'S MY LIFE VEST?!!" Brianna panicked.

Then she climbed OUT of her seat and crawled underneath it, even though the plane was already taxiing on the runway.

OMG! I almost had a heart attack when Brianna pulled out the life vest that was attached to the bottom of her seat.

"Hey! She can't do that!" Mr. Laptop Guy huffed, looking up from his computer.

"Yeah, well, you're not supposed to be on your laptop during takeoff, either!" I shot back.

But I just said it inside my head, so no one else heard it but me.

I pulled Brianna back into her seat and grabbed her seat belt.

Okay. So have you ever tried to put a seat belt on a child who is KICKING, SCREAMING, and having a TEMPER TANTRUM while wearing a LIFE VEST aboard an AIRPLANE?! . . .

BRIANNA HAS A COMPLETE MELTDOWN
ON THE PLANE!

Well, I HAVE!!

And it's pretty much . . . IMPOSSIBLE!

"Brianna, take off that LIFE VEST NOW!"
I hissed. "And get back into your seat belt!"

"But that lady said we're going to have a
WAAA-TER LAAAND-ING!" she screamed.

"We're flying from New York to Indiana. There
will NOT be a water landing," I tried to reason
with her.

"You don't know that for SURE!" she whined.

"Actually . . . I do!"

"What about lakes?! And rivers?! And . . . and . . .
SWIMMING POOLS?!" she cried.

Okay, so maybe my sister had a point, but still.

I was like, SORRY, BRIANNA!

CRASHING into a SWIMMING POOL is way better
than ANOTHER MINUTE stuck sitting next to
YOU on this PLANE!

"Look, Brianna, if you chill out, I'll let you play Princess Sugar Plum: Adventures on Baby Unicorn Island on my cell phone, okay?!"

But she didn't answer because right then the plane lifted off the ground. And our ascent into the air felt a lot like a roller coaster going up a huge hill.

That's when Brianna started to SCREAM! At the top of her lungs!

"Would you PLEASE tell her to be quiet?!" Mr. Laptop Guy grumbled.

"Sorry," I mumbled. "Brianna, hey! Look at me! We're okay! You wanted to fly! We're flying! Like . . . like fairies! Like . . . unicorns!"

"Unicorns don't FLY!" a woman muttered behind me. She was NOT helping. Thanks for NOTHING, lady!

(And I KNOW unicorns don't fly, but this was a VERY stressful situation, okay?)

"Um, is she all right?" a flight attendant said, gripping the top of Mr. Laptop Guy's seat.

I don't think she was supposed to be walking around yet, but Brianna's screams were hard to ignore.

"NOT really!" I sighed.

"Is she actually . . . wearing her LIFE VEST?!" the attendant asked in disbelief.

DUH!! This lady had a really strong grasp of the OBVIOUS!!

"I'd like a different seat," Mr. Laptop Guy snarled.

"Brianna, honey, why are you screaming?" asked my mom, who was now standing up in her row.

"Ma'am, PLEASE sit down! NOW!" the flight attendant snapped at her.

"THAT is MY daughter!" Mom shot back.

Suddenly Brianna stopped screaming and pointed out the window. "Wow! Cotton candy clouds?!"

After that, Mr. Laptop Guy switched seats with my mom, and Brianna only SCREAMED again when the plane ride got a little bumpy. . . .

And when someone flushed the toilet on the plane.

And when the flight attendant offered her apple juice because the airline didn't serve Princess Sugar Plum punch.

And when we were landing.

And when it took ten minutes to get off the plane.

And in the airport when Dad wouldn't let her RIDE on the baggage carousel with the suitcases.

I could NOT believe the moment Brianna chose to FINALLY fall asleep. In the rental car, as we were pulling into my aunt's driveway!

"Oh, she's sleeping like a little ANGEL!" my aunt gushed, gazing at her through the window.

In spite of the fact that Brianna had been acting like a TASMANIAN DEVIL in pink Barbie sneakers, my mom actually AGREED with her!

That's when I totally LOST IT!

"REALLY?! If Brianna is an ANGEL, then maybe she can FLY herself home! SORRY, people! But I will NOT be sitting next to HER on the return flight!"

But I just said that inside my head, so no one else heard it but me.

Hey, I really LOVE my little sister!

It's just that sometimes I can't help but wonder what it would be like to be an ONLY child.

Anyway, I've finally decided to break the news to Brandon about the trip to Paris when we hang out at Queasy Cheesy this weekend.

Then maybe we can both meet Chloe and Zoey at the CupCakery and tell them everything.

I've decided not to worry about those stupid photos for now.

André's last day here at WCD is tomorrow, and then he'll be going back to NHH.

So, it will be impossible for anyone to post new photos after that since we won't be around each other anymore.

I guess those HATERS will have to find something else to do.

Thank goodness all this photo drama will be over in
TWO MORE DAYS!

I just hope my BFFs don't see them before then.

Fingers crossed!

I already feel like a humongous weight has been lifted off my shoulders.

☺!!

Well, my day is pretty much RUINED ☹!

A new photo was posted two hours ago. . . .

Nikki & André snuggle and snap super-sweet selfies!

* * * * * * * * * *

CheerGirl: Awww! Don't they make
a picture-perfect couple?
LuvMyLipGloss: Nikki STILL denies they're an item,
tho. Nikki, we see you, girl!
SelfieChic: Right! She's not fooling anybody!
That chick is SO scandalous!
Flawless: I seriously can't believe she dropped Brandon
for this shallow jerk! I'm Team Brandon all the way!
Diva124: Team Brandon for life! What does André
have that he doesn't?
LuvMyLipGloss: That's easy! He's French, he's fine,
and he has tons of MONEY! All Brandon has is a
cute smile and a dusty old camera. And I totally
don't get why he LOVES hanging around stray dogs!
I mean the 4-legged ones, not Chloe, Zoey, and Nikki.
SelfieChic: LOL!!! Girlfriend, that was SHADY!

* * * * * * * * * *

That's when I stopped reading.

Those posts were CRUEL!!

I sighed and blinked back my tears.

423

Then I studied the photo carefully, trying my best to remember when André and I may have taken any selfies together.

Based on the outfit I was wearing, this had to have been taken on Tuesday.

That's when I suddenly remembered that Chloe, Zoey, André, and I had taken a selfie together on that day.

But it appeared that Chloe and Zoey had been completely cropped out of the photo.

Obviously, someone wanted it to look like André and I were taking selfies together because we were totally into each other.

Which is a BIG FAT LIE!!

I was SO . . .

ANGRY ☹!

But not nearly as ANGRY as I was about the photo that was just posted ten minutes ago. . . .

Nikki & André share a pastry!

* * * * * * * * * *

SelfieChic: OMG! This is SOOO romantic!

Diva124: Well, it's quite obvious they're serious about each other.

Flawless: Nikki! How could you?!

LuvMyLipGloss: Just wait until Brandon finds out. Watching her messy love life unfold will be like watching a train wreck. I am totally LOVING IT!

SelfieChic: Me too! Things are getting good! I've got my bowl of popcorn ready!

LuvMyLipGloss: I've got candy and my 3-D glasses on! LOL!

CheerGirl: Um . . . I think you two are enjoying this a little too much.

Diva124: Why am I suddenly hungry for a warm cinnamon bun with cream cheese frosting?

Flawless: Me too! Let's meet at the CupCakery after school.

* * * * * * * * * *

I stopped reading and shoved my cell phone back into my purse.

426

I wanted to . . .

SCREEEEEAM ☹!!

André and I each had our OWN cinnamon roll!

But for some reason, only ONE was shown in the photo!

MINE ☹!!

There was NO WAY we were just sitting there in the library like a bride and groom sharing a piece of wedding cake!

Hey, I barely even KNOW the guy!!

To make things even worse, it feels like the entire school is GOSSIPING about me.

Well, most of the kids in the CCP (Cute, Cool, and Popular) clique, anyway.

MacKenzie and her friends were whispering about me while I was at my locker.

My stomach feels so QUEASY, I could throw up on MacKenzie's really cute gold designer platform sandals.

If I wasn't so WORRIED about Brandon seeing those photos, assuming the worst, getting his feelings hurt, and then NEVER speaking to me again, I'd rush down to the office, call my mom, and go HOME!

But instead I plan to go straight to BIO and WARN Brandon about those photos!

Before it's too late!

☹!

THURSDAY—3:30 P.M.
IN THE JANITOR'S CLOSET

Right now I'm in the janitor's closet, writing this and trying not to have a complete MELTDOWN!

OMG! MacKenzie Hollister is . . .

PURE EVIL ☹!

HOW evil is she?!!

She's SO evil that if I was in the HOSPITAL, she'd UNPLUG my LIFE SUPPORT to charge her CELL PHONE!

As soon as I finished my last diary entry, I grabbed my books, stopped by André's locker (hey, he's part of my job duties!), and rushed straight to bio.

But, unfortunately, I had arrived just seconds TOO LATE. . . .

429

MACKENZIE SHOWS BRANDON
THE PICS OF ANDRÉ AND ME!

I just stood there FREAKING OUT as Brandon scrolled through the photos. He looked shocked, surprised, and hurt! All at the same time. . . .

BRANDON LOOKS AT THE PICS!

Right then all I wanted to do was dig a really deep hole right next to my desk, CRAWL into it, and DIE!!

Once class started, I could practically feel Brandon staring at the back of my head.

But whenever I turned around to make eye contact, he just gazed blankly at his bio book.

Of course MacKenzie sat there with a big fat SMIRK on her face.

She was SO proud of herself for pretty much DESTROYING my friendship with Brandon.

I wanted to walk right up to her and say, "Congratulations, MacKenzie!" and give her a high five!

In the FACE. With a CHAIR!

Just kidding ☺!

NOT 😞!

Seriously! That girl is lucky I'm a very peaceful and nonviolent person.

I just totally ignored her when she started EYEBALLING me all EVIL-LIKE. . . .

MACKENZIE, EYEBALLING ME
ALL EVIL-LIKE

I mean, WHO does THAT?!!

As soon as class was over, Brandon grabbed his backpack and quickly strode past me and out of the room.

Practically everyone in class had heard the latest gossip and was STARING at us.

"Brandon, wait! I really need to talk to you!" I said, following him out into the hall. "Privately. Can we meet at your locker after school?"

"Actually, Nikki, I'm supposed to work on the Fuzzy Friends website with some volunteers after school. I've been staying up really late all week, and it's not even half finished. And now my homework is piling up," he said, staring at the floor.

I had to admit, he looked exhausted.

I hadn't noticed the dark circles under his eyes until now.

"Well, how about tomorrow morning?" I asked.

434

"I'm coming to school an hour early tomorrow. But I'll be busy in the library, trying to finish up all my homework that was due YESTERDAY and TODAY," he muttered in frustration.

"Can you at least give me a minute or two?" I practically begged. "I mean, if you have time. . . ."

"The real question is, do YOU have time?" Brandon said, finally looking at me. "Apparently, you've been really busy lately with your NEW school project!"

"School project?! WHAT school project?" I asked, confused.

Suddenly Brandon narrowed his eyes and stared behind me.

"Here, Nicole," André said, handing me my backpack. "We'd better get going or we'll be late for class. Oh . . . hello, Brandon."

"NICOLE?! Who's . . . Nicole?" Brandon asked, staring at me, then André, and then back at me. "Never mind. I gotta go. Later."

He sighed, thrust his hands deep into his pockets, turned, and trudged away.

"What's wrong with HIM?" André shrugged. "He's acting like his BEST FRIEND just DIED!"

"Actually, SHE DID!" I sighed, blinking back tears as I watched Brandon disappear down the hall.

☹!

OMG! All that drama in BIO yesterday was . . .

HORRIFIC!

I had no idea Brandon was feeling overwhelmed.

He's been spending so much time working on the Fuzzy Friends project that he's fallen behind on his homework and started to struggle at school.

And if all that isn't EXHAUSTING enough, he's ALSO been coming to MY house TWICE a week to train Daisy.

I honestly can't blame Brandon for feeling a little insecure about OUR friendship when I've been spending so much time with André.

Those pics of André and me probably felt like a huge SLAP in the face and pushed him over the edge.

And now I can't get him out of my mind! He looked so SAD just sitting there alone. . . .

BRANDON AT SCHOOL

Obviously, whoever posted those photos is trying to hurt him AND damage our friendship.

But I have to admit, I'm ALSO responsible. I was SO self-absorbed in my own little world, worrying about my own personal problems, that I'd basically ignored Brandon.

I felt really AWFUL that I'd let my friend down like that ☹! I didn't have a choice but to try to make it up to him, some way, somehow.

Brandon had asked me to draw some of the puppies that had recently been placed by Fuzzy Friends, but instead I'd gotten sidetracked with my student ambassador duties.

So last night, after I completed my homework, I worked on those puppy drawings for HOURS! I didn't finish until after midnight.

I realize I'm the LAST person Brandon wants to talk to right now. So I decided to write him a short letter.

I plan to give it to him along with the puppy drawings when I see him at school today. . . .

Hi,

Please let me know what you think about the four pics. I think they're DEFINITELY going to get a lot of attention online!

BTW, can we hang out later to talk? It's about something kind of important. Okay, VERY important! So important that I've been trying to tell you about it for the past week but couldn't.

It was hard finding the right time since we've both been insanely busy. So let's hang out this Saturday! Does 1:00 p.m. at Queasy Cheesy work for you? Shoot me a text and let me know. After the stressful week we've had, it'll be fun to just eat and chillax with you!

Nikki

I folded the letter, tucked it into an envelope, and scribbled Brandon's name on it.

It's hard to believe that today is André's last day at WCD! The week went by so fast. In spite of all the DRAMA his visit created, I really like him and consider him a new friend. But, unfortunately,

I'm feeling more confused than ever about having to choose between the Bad Boyz tour and the trip to Paris. So I decided to write a letter to André. . . .

Hi,

I can't believe how fast this week went by! The good news is that you survived it ☺.

Now comes the awkward part. . . . I wanted to let you know that I'm still thinking about what we discussed. And, to be honest, I just don't know how I feel yet.

Having to choose between two things I really care about is A LOT of pressure! Half of me wants to stick with what's familiar and makes me happy. And the other half of me wants something new, adventurous, and exciting.

I'm SO torn!! Maybe I'm afraid of disappointing people. Or maybe I'm just scared of making a commitment. I'm going to need more time to figure stuff out.

I hope you understand! When I make my final decision, I'll definitely let you know. Regardless of

what I decide, I'd still like to be friends if that's
okay with you! Hopefully, I'll see you around.

Nikki

P.S. Here is that gift card for a FREE Queasy
Cheesy pizza. ENJOY ☺!

I tucked the letter into a second envelope and
scribbled André's name on it. Then I stuck both
letters and the drawings into a folder and placed
everything inside my backpack.

It feels like I'm FINALLY getting my life back under
control. The good news is that on Monday my schedule
will be back to normal and I'll have two classes and lunch
with Chloe and Zoey again! SQUEEEE ☺!

OMG! They're NOT going to believe all the SHADY stuff
MacKenzie did to me this week. I can't wait to tell them.

But, most important, I'm REALLY going to need my
BFFs to help me patch things up with Brandon. ☺!!

442

FRIDAY—9:55 A.M.
AT MY LOCKER

I arrived at school this morning fifteen minutes early, just as I had planned.

I was hoping it was enough time to find Brandon and give him the artwork and the letter.

It was the first step toward rebuilding our friendship.

Yesterday he'd mentioned that he was going to be in the library trying to catch up on homework, so my plan was to start there.

Since it was a warm and breezy day, I decided to stop in the girls' bathroom just to make sure my hair wasn't windblown and I didn't have any food stuck in my teeth.

But as soon as I stepped inside, my stomach started to churn so badly, I thought for sure I was going to lose my taco breakfast bagel. . . .

WHY?! Because MacKenzie was at the mirror, slathering on nine layers of lip gloss. . . .

I RUN INTO MACKENZIE
IN THE GIRLS' BATHROOM!

I didn't have any proof! But I was VERY sure she had tried to destroy my friendship with Brandon by posting those photoshopped pics online and then making sure he saw them.

I just stood there staring at her.

"Hi, Nikki! I LOVED your pics online! Go right ahead and use the mirror. If you're going to be TWO-FACED, at least make ONE of them pretty!"

"I know you put those pics online, so just admit it, MacKenzie!" I shot back.

"So what if I did! You should thank me. Now you're slightly more popular at this school than the toilet bowl stains! Congratulations, hon!"

"MacKenzie, CYBERBULLYING is WRONG! I'd love to try to EXPLAIN that concept to you in a way you'd understand, but I don't have any SOCK PUPPETS, CHEERIOS, and CRAYONS!"

MacKenzie turned and glared at me.

"Nikki, I am SO sick of you! Everything is handed to you on a silver platter, and you don't deserve any of it. I should be going on that Bad Boyz tour! And as soon as you dump your little friends to go hang out in Paris with André, that lead singer SPOT is all MINE! To be honest, I don't get what André or Brandon see in you. They should be obsessed with ME! I guess you're just irresistibly ADORABLE and DUMB like a little puppy!"

"Wait a minute. You're doing all this just to go on tour?! Do you even realize you're HURTING other people? Like my FRIENDS?!" I exclaimed.

"Sorry, Nikki! You must be mistaking me for someone who actually CARES! Is your little bathroom DRAMA going to have an intermission soon? Because I need to pee!"

It was like MacKenzie had NOT heard a single word I'd said. She was HOPELESS!

"Listen, Nikki! Could you do me a big favor and go stand inside a stall until I leave? Your ugly dress is clashing with my lip gloss, and it's giving me a MIGRAINE!"

When you encounter a big PILE of CRAZY, sometimes it's best not to waste your time and energy trying to REASON with it. So I turned and walked away.

It was WAY more important that I try to find Brandon and give him the artwork.

But by the time I got to the library door, I suddenly realized I didn't have my backpack.

JUST GREAT ☹!!

I had left it in the BATHROOM!!

With . . . MACKENZIE HOLLISTER ☹!!

I turned around and sprinted down the hall, back to the bathroom. I just KNEW my backpack was history!

But MacKenzie must not have noticed it under the counter, because it was STILL there. . . .

I FIND MY BACKPACK!!

I looked inside and saw my purse, phone, and book.

My artwork was in my folder, and when I peeked inside the envelopes, my letters were still there.

WHEW ☺!!

I hurried back to the library again.

My heart actually skipped a beat when I spotted Brandon sitting at a back table, hunched over a notebook.

"What's up, Brandon?" I said cheerfully. "I have a surprise! It's for the Fuzzy Friends website."

He didn't answer or even look at me. Maybe he was more upset at me than I thought.

I just froze, not having the slightest idea what to do next.

"Um, Brandon, are you okay?"

That's when I finally realized he was even more exhausted than yesterday. The poor guy should've just stayed home from school.

I didn't have the heart to disturb him. So I tiptoed over to him and very quietly left my puppy drawings and my letter on the table right next to his notebook. . . .

AN EXHAUSTED BRANDON,
SLEEPING IN THE LIBRARY!

450

I couldn't help but feel a little sorry for Brandon.

He was SO passionate about Fuzzy Friends and animals (like my CRAZY dog, Daisy) that he had completely worn himself out.

I wanted to wake him up, thank him for all his hard work, and give him a great big HUG. But I didn't. I just stood there staring at him.

Suddenly it became very clear to me how I wanted to spend my summer.

André is a smart, handsome, and fascinating guy. And Paris is one of the most exciting cities in the world.

But I'd much rather spend the summer hanging out with my kindhearted and dorky CRUSH, Brandon.

I can't wait to tell him just how I feel.

451

Okay, I think this is probably going to be my LONGEST diary entry EVER!

First of all, I didn't have the slightest idea if Brandon was even going to show up at Queasy Cheesy.

I'd asked him in my letter to text me to let me know if Saturday at 1:00 p.m. was a good time, but he never responded.

I was starting to worry that maybe he was still MAD at me or something. Although I couldn't blame him.

If I had treated MYSELF the way I'd treated Brandon, I definitely would have UNFRIENDED myself on FACEBOOK!

I arrived at Queasy Cheesy fifteen minutes early and was a nervous wreck. But soon 1:00 p.m. had come and gone.

That's when it became VERY clear.

MY CRUSH HAD DITCHED ME!! ...

ME, HAVING A VERY SERIOUS CRUSH-ITIS CRISIS

<u>OMG!</u> My <u>WORST</u> fear had come true.

I was suffering from that very dangerous crush-itis complication that Chloe and Zoey had WARNED me about!

I totally lost it and had a massive meltdown right there at my table. While everyone in the restaurant stared at me.

Finally, my waitress came over and smiled at me sympathetically. "Dear, you've been waiting here for quite a while. Would you like to place your order now?"

"Um . . . I think I'll just wait a few minutes longer," I muttered.

"Well, suit yourself, honey. But, personally, I DON'T think HE'S coming! You're probably just wasting your time," she said, and walked away.

I could <u>NOT</u> believe my waitress actually said that to me! <u>HOW RUDE</u> ☹!!

WHY was she all up in my personal business like that?! I had never seen that lady before in my life!

I seriously thought about complaining to the management.

But then I remembered the Queasy Cheesy pizza gift cards that my dad had given me.

If I made a big stink about the waitress, it might end up damaging my dad's business relationship.

I'd completely given up hope and was looking at the takeout menu when I heard a familiar voice. . . .

"SORRY I'M LATE! I HOPE I DIDN'T KEEP YOU WAITING TOO LONG!"

Lucky me! I won't be leaving here in tears with a broken heart, munching on a takeout order of wing-dings after all, I thought happily ☺!

I looked up, HOPING to see my crush, Brandon. . . .

BUT IT WAS ANDRÉ!

"Oh! Hi, André!" I said, trying not to sound as disappointed as I felt. "How are you? Um . . . what are YOU doing here?"

"Well, I was invited by a very special person!" he said, with a huge smile plastered across his face. "I'm here to wish her happiness and help celebrate her success!"

I couldn't help but notice the balloons and CupCakery box he was holding.

"So, you're here for a party or something?" I asked, a little confused.

André seemed a little too old to be invited to a kiddie-themed birthday party at Queasy Cheesy. But hey, who was I to judge?!

Or maybe he was here for his OWN birthday.

"OMG, André! Is it YOUR birthday today? If so, the least I can do is, um . . . buy you some Queasy Cheesy tokens for the game room. I need to warn you that the popcorn is a little stale, and, whatever you do, DON'T go into the ball pit. My little sister, Brianna, said a kid threw up in it the last time we were here."

457

André laughed. "You have such a wicked sense of humor, Nicole. But it's NOT my birthday. Oh, I almost forgot. Here! These are for YOU!"

He handed me the mini bouquet of balloons and the CupCakery box.

"I brought you French pastries! They're just a small taste of the totally AMAZING things you'll experience during a summer in PARIS!" he said wistfully.

"André, you DIDN'T have to do this! I was just doing my job as a student ambassador. I mean, it was MANDATORY. I didn't have a choice."

"But I DO have a choice! And I want you to have them." He smiled. "I'll go ask the waitress for plates. You should try a chocolate croissant while they're still warm. I'll be right back!"

"But what about that party you said you were invited to? I don't want you to miss it because of me," I protested as he walked away and disappeared in the crowded restaurant.

Curious, I opened the box and peeked inside at the pastries. They looked delish!

I was startled by a voice directly behind me, and I turned to see a guy staring at me. . . .

NIKKI?! WHAT'S UP? I DIDN'T EXPECT TO SEE YOU HERE!

QUEASY CHEESY

IT WAS BRANDON!!

"OMG! Brandon, you're HERE!" I gushed. "I'm SO happy to see you!"

"Thanks. I'm happy to see you, too!" He blushed.

"But what are you doing with that pizza? I've barely looked at the menu," I said.

"It's my takeout order. I just stopped by to pick it up. I'm still working on the website, so I'll eat it at Fuzzy Friends," Brandon explained.

"You want to eat the pizza at Fuzzy Friends instead of HERE?! Well . . . okay. That sounds fine to me." I shrugged. "Actually, it would give us more privacy to talk. I'll let the waitress know."

"Thanks for the pizza and for the puppy drawings. They're AWESOME, Nikki! I planned to text you about them later today."

"I'm glad I could help out," I said. "Anyway, now that you're finally here, we REALLY need to talk. I tried to explain everything in my letter."

"Yeah, I got your letter," Brandon sighed. "I have to admit, after reading it I'm a little—no, I'm VERY confused."

"Just have a seat and we'll talk. I'll explain everything, including the photo drama, okay?"

"Sure. Although, to be honest, I think I owe YOU an apology," Brandon said shyly as he brushed his shaggy bangs out of his eyes. "You know, for the way I've been acting lately."

"Actually, I owe YOU an apology, Brandon."

"Listen, I agree we should talk. But I really need to go pay for this pizza with a gift card. I wouldn't want them to think I was trying to STEAL it!" Brandon joked.

"Yeah, my dad gave me some pizza gift cards too." I laughed. "I'm going to use one to pay for this meal."

"Okay, I'll be right back," Brandon said as he walked toward the checkout line.

That's when André returned.

"We're all set. The waitress is going to bring over some plates," he said.

"Good! So, um, thanks for the pastries and balloons. It's been nice talking to you, André."

Then, for some reason, he sat down at my table, picked up the menu, and started reading it. Then he kind of stared at me and smiled.

"So, I read your letter, Nicole. I realize we've only known each other for a week, but it feels like a year. I honestly never thought you'd feel the same way about ME that I feel about YOU!"

"OMG! André, YOU'RE having second thoughts about US spending the summer in Paris together TOO?! I'm SO relieved! This is really good news! I was hoping you'd understand!"

"Um, actually, I DON'T understand!" André mumbled. "I'm a little confused."

"Just like I said in my letter, if I change my mind, I'll let you know! Now, I think you should get to that party. I'd hate for you to miss out!"

"You keep talking about a party. WHAT party?!" André asked, getting a little annoyed.

"The one you said you were invited to. Don't you remember?"

That's when I heard someone clear their throat rather loudly.

It was Brandon!

He was back, and he did NOT look happy to see André sitting there. And André did NOT look very happy to see Brandon.

They both just stared at each other for what seemed like FOREVER.

Then the three of us had a really deep and meaningful conversation. . . .

"So, Brandon," I said cheerfully. "Why don't you, um . . . have a seat?"

"I CAN'T!" Brandon grumbled. "André is in my SEAT! Again! It's becoming a really BAD habit, dude! What's up with that?!"

"Hi, Brandon!" André said drily. "What are YOU doing here?"

"No, the question is, WHAT are YOU doing in MY seat?" Brandon muttered.

I could not believe Brandon and André were acting SO immature. They were starting to get on my last nerve.

"Actually, André just stopped by to say hello. He's here for a birthday party," I explained.

"There. Is. No. PARTY!" André said under his breath.

Brandon narrowed his eyes at André. "So, the balloon says 'Congrats!!' What's the occasion?"

André folded his arms and grinned at Brandon.

"Nikki was awarded the trip to PARIS! It'll be fourteen days in mid-July, and I've volunteered to show her around the city! Didn't she tell you?!"

Brandon looked like he'd just gotten hit in the face with a dodgeball.

"Um . . . NO! She DIDN'T tell me! But what she DID tell ME was that she was going on the Bad Boyz tour the entire month of July, and I believed her. Although now I don't know WHAT to believe. Nikki, your letter is starting to make a lot more sense. . . ." Brandon trailed off as a wave of hurt washed over his face.

"Actually, André, I haven't had a chance to tell Brandon about the Paris trip yet!" I said.

"OOPS!" André shrugged. "SORRY!"

"Nikki, why didn't you tell me?" Brandon asked. "That's pretty important news! And it impacts ALL of our summer plans."

"Well, I tried to tell you, Chloe, and Zoey on Wednesday. And I tried to tell you again on Thursday, but you wouldn't even talk to me! That's why I wrote the letter," I explained.

"Okay, Nikki. I just have one question," Brandon said quietly as he stared at the floor. "Did you really mean what you said in that letter? I need to know that."

"Yes, Brandon, I meant every WORD of it. And I meant every WORD of the letter I gave to you, André. I would really appreciate it if you BOTH would let me make my OWN decisions. Just try to get along and stop acting like four-year-olds."

"You're right, Nikki," Brandon said solemnly. "I just want you to be HAPPY! And if it means Paris, then that's what I want for you. Listen, I'd better get going. This pizza is getting cold. So I'll . . . um . . . see you around. Maybe."

He turned and walked toward the door.

"Listen, Brandon. You don't have to leave. We still need to talk. At least I owe you an explanation. WAIT!" I said as I blinked back tears.

But Brandon just ignored me and kept walking.

He stopped at the door, glanced at me over his shoulder, and then opened it to leave.

At that moment it was quite obvious to me that our friendship, or whatever we had, was officially over ☹.

OMG! I can't believe it's after midnight. I'm mentally and physically EXHAUSTED just writing about all this stuff.

I'll think I'll finish this diary entry . . .

TOMORROW!

Right now I need to get some sleep!

☹!!

I still haven't quite recovered from all the drama at Queasy Cheesy. It was UNREAL!

Unfortunately, I won't have much time to write in my diary today because my mom is making me take Brianna to see _Princess Sugar Plum Saves Baby Unicorn Island: Part 9_ ☹!

After that I plan to watch a marathon session of _My Very Rich and Trashy Life!_ reruns, eat dinner, do my homework, and then go to bed.

Now, where did I leave off? . . . I was practically in tears at Queasy Cheesy as I watched Brandon walk away. He glanced sadly at me over his shoulder and then opened the door.

That's when my BFFs, CHLOE and ZOEY, came STORMING into the restaurant, YELLING like their HAIR was on FIRE!! . . .

MY BFFS, CHLOE AND ZOEY,
ARRIVING AT QUEASY CHEESY

"OMG! Thank goodness we found you, Nikki!" Chloe shrieked, out of breath.

"We called your mom, and she told us you were here!" Zoey shouted excitedly.

WHAT in the world is going on? I wondered. Then they each grabbed Brandon by an arm and practically dragged him back to my table.

"Listen, Chloe and Zoey," Brandon grumbled, "the last thing I want to do is interrupt Nikki's date. So I was just leaving. . . ."

"BRANDON! SIT DOWN!!" Chloe and Zoey both yelled at him.

Brandon blinked in surprise, pulled up a chair from a nearby table, and quickly sat down.

"Listen, guys," André said, "I know you're really good friends and all. But Nicole personally invited ME here to discuss our summer plans. I think you need to respect our privacy."

472

That's when Chloe totally lost it. "Listen, Mr. Cutie Pants! You can talk to Nicole all you want. But stay away from our BFF, Nikki! I'm warning you! I know karate, kung fu, judo, tae kwon do, and at least five other dangerous words!" she growled.

"You tell him, girlfriend!" Zoey said. "And I'VE got . . . ! Wait, I know I put that thing in here somewhere," she said, digging around inside her purse.

Suddenly she whipped out her cell phone.

Just GREAT ☹! Chloe and Zoey barged in like a herd of wild buffalo and threatened my new friend, André, with violence!

JUST to take a few more cute SELFIES with him?!

I was SO disgusted!

Zoey tapped her phone a few times. "And I've got . . . THIS! An incriminating PHOTO!"

She shoved it right in André's face. "Can you explain THIS, André?!" Zoey shouted.

André stared at it and furrowed his brow.

"Um . . . it looks like a girl in pink pajamas with a mud mask on, dancing while singing into a hairbrush?" He shrugged.

"Oh, wait! That's me! Wrong photo!" She giggled nervously as she tapped her phone again.

Then she shoved her phone into André's face again. "Okay! Explain THIS!"

"Um . . . it's a little old lady with a party hat on, blowing out candles on a birthday cake?" he said.

"Oops! That's my grandma's seventy-fifth birthday party! Wrong photo again. This STUPID phone is so touch sensitive," she grumbled.

I just rolled my eyes. Brandon shook his head in disbelief. André looked a little bored.

"Okay, let's try this ONE LAST time! Explain . . . THIS!" Zoey snarled.

André glanced at the phone with a smirk on his face. But it quickly melted into concern. . . .

ZOEY, INTERROGATING ANDRÉ

<u>Poor André, I thought. It looked like my BFFs had</u>
<u>finally discovered those online photos of us.</u>

<u>Queasy Cheesy is known for its entertainment that</u>
<u>features Queasy the Mouse and his rock band of</u>
<u>animatronic animal pals. NOT my over-the-top</u>
<u>middle school DRAMA!</u>

<u>But people were staring and eating popcorn ☹!</u>

<u>"Nikki, we're here to warn you that you're eating</u>
<u>pizza with a DIRTY RAT!" Zoey said loudly.</u>

<u>Just at that moment, Queasy the Mouse was</u>
<u>waddling by with a tray of pizza and heard her.</u>
<u>He stopped in his tracks and sadly hung his head.</u>

<u>"Come on, Zoey! Queasy's a mouse, not a rat. And</u>
<u>he's not THAT dirty," I argued. "Rodents have</u>
<u>feelings too, you know."</u>

<u>"Actually, I wasn't talking about Queasy!" Zoey</u>
<u>said. "Um . . . sorry about that!" She gave the</u>
<u>costumed mouse a sheepish grin. "We GOOD?!"</u>

Queasy gave her a nod and a thumbs-up and happily waddled away.

"I was talking about the two-faced WEASEL over there!" Zoey said, pointing.

I thought she was throwing shade at Willy the Weasel, who played guitar on the Queasy Cheesy stage. But she was pointing straight at André, who stared back with a worried look on his face.

"André?!" I uttered in shock. "Zoey, what are you talking about? You're making a BIG mistake."

Chloe tapped Zoey's shoulder. "I'll take it from here. I got this!" she said gruffly, like the bad cop. Uh-oh, I thought. Chloe is my BFF and all, but sometimes that girl can be so . . . EXTRA!

"So, Chloe and Zoey, would you like one? They're delish!" André said nervously as he offered them his box of French pastries.

"Dude, the ONLY reason we're here is to . . .

TAKE. YOU. DOWN!" Chloe said, wagging her finger in his face. "Nobody messes with our BFF! Even if they've got delicious, melt-in-your-mouth chocolate pastries that are still warm and smell heavenly!"

She snatched the box of pastries from André and shoved one into her mouth. . . .

CHLOE, EATING MY CHOCOLATE PASTRIES!

"I'm confiscating these for . . . um . . . evidence! I need to taste test each one for safety reasons!" Chloe muttered with her mouth full.

"Chloe, CHILLAX!" I shouted. "Leave André alone! And PLEASE tell me what's going on!!"

"Nikki, someone has been posting altered photos of you online to create scandalous gossip about you shamelessly flirting with André," Zoey explained. "And they've been posting nasty comments on the message boards about ALL of us. They actually called you, Zoey, and me DOGS!"

"We are NOT dogs!" Chloe said angrily, her hands on her hips. "Zoey and I only got FLEAS that one time we helped Brandon wash dogs at Fuzzy Friends. But it wasn't HIS fault WE forgot to use the flea dip!"

"Thank you for coming here to tell me all this stuff. But I already know about it," I said.

"YOU DO?!" Chloe and Zoey gasped in surprise.

"Yeah! Brandon does too. And you just told André. I think SelfieChic is Tiffany and MacKenzie is LuvMyLipGloss. MacKenzie pretty much admitted to me she posted the pics. But I'm sure she's going to LIE like a rug if we report her to Principal Winston for cyberbullying. We're going to need more PROOF!"

"Well, here's another piece of the puzzle for you!" Zoey said as she showed Brandon and me that photo on her phone.

I'd assumed it was one of the photos of André and me online, but it WASN'T!

OMG! I could NOT believe my eyes! It was . . .

SHOCKING!

The four of us just GLARED at André like he was something nasty Daisy had left behind the couch.

"Listen, that photo is NOT what it seems. Nicole,

you've got to b-believe me! I c-can explain!" André stammered.

"Okay, André. You have exactly ONE minute," I said, trying to remain calm. "Start EXPLAINING!"

Maybe there WAS a perfectly innocent explanation for what we saw in that photo ☺! But from the looks of it, probably NOT ☹!

UH-OH! My mom just called me.

I have to stop writing now.

Time to go on an EXCITING trip to Baby Unicorn Island for yet another CAPTIVATING adventure with Princess Sugar Plum and my bratty little sister.

WHY was I NOT born an only child?!

☹!!

I thought I knew André pretty well. He seemed like a really nice guy, but I guess I was wrong.

I had been happy to hang out with him because he said he'd just started attending North Hampton Hills and didn't have any friends.

He had also confessed that he hated being the "new kid" and was really worried about fitting in.

I felt the EXACT same way when I first came to Westchester Country Day Middle School.

OMG! It was HORRIBLE! The first few weeks of school, I wandered the halls like a ZOMBIE!

No one ever talked to me and I sat alone at lunch every single day. MacKenzie always went out of her way to make my life MISERABLE!

So Chloe's cell phone pic kind of blew my mind! . . .

ANDRÉ AT THE CUPCAKERY WITH
MACKENZIE AND TIFFANY?!

I don't know why, but BOTH MacKenzie and Tiffany HATE MY GUTS ☹!!

And now it appears that André is FRIENDS with them AND has been HELPING them post photos and nasty comments online.

Chloe and Zoey had been at the CupCakery earlier that day and had seen the three of them together. They'd snapped that pic just for me.

I felt numb. I was so hurt and upset, I wanted to CRY!! I really thought he was my friend.

André was talking, but I wasn't really listening.

". . . so I just sat down at their table for a minute just to see what they were up to and say hi. Then I grabbed the pastries and came straight over here. And that's the truth, Nicole!"

The four of us just stared at André silently. Then Chloe cleared her throat. "André, would you like to know what we're thinking right now?"

He smiled weakly and looked hopeful. "Sure, Chloe. I'd love to hear what you have to say."

"ANDRÉ, THAT'S THE MOST RIDICULOUS STORY WE'VE EVER HEARD AND A COMPLETE PACK OF LIES, YOU PATHETIC CYBERBULLY!" she yelled.

"Listen, I'm sorry you guys don't believe me. But that's NOT going to stop me from doing the right thing!" André said, getting up to leave. "And, Nicole, I'll always . . ." He looked at Brandon and stopped midsentence.

I don't know why, but I suddenly felt REALLY confused. What if André was telling the truth?

We watched as André walked to the door.

He glanced sadly at me over his shoulder and then opened the door.

That's when MacKenzie and Tiffany came barreling through the door, yelling at the top of their lungs like they had lost their minds. . . .

"ANDRÉ! YOU THIEF!! YOU ARE SO BUSTED!" MacKenzie yelled.

"GIVE ME BACK MY PHONE! NOW!" Tiffany screamed. "I KNOW YOU TOOK IT!"

They each grabbed him by an arm and practically dragged him back to our table. My friends and I just stared at them, speechless. WHAT was going on?!

The biggest question was, when had MacKenzie and Tiffany become members of the I HATE ANDRÉ CLUB? They were ALL at the CupCakery just an hour ago, CANOODLING like BFFs. Something was very FISHY!

"You know what, Tiffany? I DON'T believe you for one second!" I said. "YOU stole Mr. Winter's lesson plan book and then told him that I did it, remember? And NOW you're saying André stole your phone. You may not be a pathological LIAR, but I bet you're really close!"

"Tiffany, I totally agree with Nikki," Brandon said.

"I HATE to admit it, but I don't think André stole your phone! He may be a cold, deceitful, backstabbing cyberbully, but I don't think he's a dirty, rotten, sleazy THIEF."

Chloe and Zoey nodded in agreement. . . .

IT FELT LIKE ANDRÉ WAS ON TRIAL AND WE WERE THE JUDGE AND JURY!

But what happened next ALMOST made my head
EXPLODE!

"Actually . . . I AM a dirty, rotten, sleazy THIEF!"
André confessed, like it was NOT a big deal.

THEN HE ACTUALLY PULLED TIFFANY'S
CELL PHONE OUT OF HIS BACK POCKET!

Everyone gasped! I could not believe my eyes!

"See, Nikki?! I told you André was shady!" Chloe
exclaimed. "Someone call the POLICE! Quick!"

"Just let me explain, okay?" André pleaded. "While
I was at the CupCakery picking up the pastries, I
overheard Tiffany and MacKenzie talking about
the photos they'd posted online. I saw them posting
nasty comments on some website using Tiffany's
phone. So I just kind of borrowed it so I'd have
proof of what they were doing. I'll give it back to
her later today."

"Dude, isn't that illegal?" Brandon said.

"How do we know you didn't STEAL those pastries, too?!" Chloe shrieked. "OMG! I've been eating STOLEN property! I'm going to JAIL!"

"You're NOT going to get away with taking MY phone, André!" Tiffany yelled. "You mess with me and you're going to be in BIG trouble! Give it back right now! Or I'm . . . I'm telling MOM!"

"No you're not, Tiffany!" André shot back. "Because . . . I'M TELLING MOM!! Sorry, but you're BUSTED! For cyberbullying people again! I have all the proof I need right here. Mom will probably ground you for half the summer and make you do community service at the senior citizens center. Just like last time!"

"André, don't you DARE tell Mom! PLEEEASE!" Tiffany whined. "I HATE volunteering at the senior citizens center. I'd rather EAT five tubes of denture cream and DROWN myself in a bucket of PRUNE JUICE than go back there!"

"Hold up! Hold up! Hold up!" Zoey interrupted.

"Tiffany, Imma let you finish!" she said, like that famous rapper. "But . . . ANDRÉ IS YOUR BROTHER?!!"

My head was SPINNING!

"I'm her STEPBROTHER!" André answered. "My mother is married to Tiffany's father."

That's when my head actually EXPLODED!! KA-BOOM!!

"Who needs pizza?! This is an all-you-can-eat DRAMA buffet!" Zoey said, shaking her head.

"Tiffany, what you and MacKenzie did was just . . . CRUEL!" I was SO angry, I could, um . . . SPIT!

"OMG! Are you seriously trying to shame me for cyberbullying right now?" Tiffany scoffed. "My cell phone has been STOLEN and my summer has been RUINED! That makes ME the real VICTIM here! And HOW am I going to get my hourly SELFIE fix with no cell phone, Nikki?!!"

"Sorry, girl, but I'm not sorry!" I shot back.

"Tiffany, I'm shocked! How could you be so mean to Nikki?! Dorks have feelings too, you know!" MacKenzie said, creeping toward the door. "I'd love to stay longer, but I need to go home and wash my hair and get my beauty sleep! Toodles!"

"Oh, no you don't!" Tiffany grabbed MacKenzie's arm. "Shampoo isn't going to fix your raggedy split ends. You need a car wash! Besides, how could you bail on your BFF like this?!"

"Well, no shade, Tiff! But I don't really know you like that!" MacKenzie said coldly. "Besides, Jessica is my real BFF, not you. So whatever."

"Fine! Who needs a BFF like you, anyway?" Tiffany spat. "And, girlfriend, you don't need beauty sleep to fix that face! You need to HIBERNATE! Until next SPRING! And before you leave, why don't you tell everyone how you snuck into Nikki's backpack and SWITCHED Brandon's and André's letters?! If I'm going DOWN, you're coming WITH me!"

MacKenzie just glared at her. "Tiffany, all that gossip about you being a ruthless backstabber is true! My cell phone BATTERY lasts LONGER than your FRIENDSHIPS!"

MACKENZIE AND TIFFANY
HAVE A MEAN GIRL SPAT!

Then MacKenzie turned to me. "Nikki, you were right about Tiffany. She IS a bigger liar than I am! I feel SO sorry for her. I'd hug her, but I don't want to get DUMB on my arms! I'd much rather be friends with you."

It was quite obvious that MacKenzie was just trying to weasel her way out of the mess she and Tiffany had made.

André had been oddly quiet.

"Um . . . Tiffany, what did you mean about the letters being switched? So I got the one meant for Brandon?"

"That's right, Romeo. Don't tell me you thought Nikki was really into you!" Tiffany laughed cruelly. "She didn't invite YOU to Queasy Cheesy, she invited Brandon! MacKenzie has the IQ of an orange crayon, but she played you both like a video game. You lovesick losers will fall for anything!"

Both André and Brandon looked shocked.

So THAT was why they'd both been acting so strange ever since they'd gotten my letters.

I felt really bad for them both.

"Listen, guys, I'm really sorry about the letters. You didn't deserve that, and I apologize."

"No need to apologize, Nicole," André replied. "I'm sorry if I was a bit, um . . . overbearing. I was just a little confused, I guess."

"Same here," Brandon said. "If anything, WE both owe YOU an apology, Nikki!"

"Guys, you know what I WANT more than an apology? For you two to get along and STOP fighting over SEATS!" I teased.

"Listen, André, I was wrong about you," Brandon said. "You're not a cyberbully or a thief. You're really a cool DUDE! For a French guy, anyway."

"Likewise, my friend." André smiled back. "For you

to have figured all that out means you're pretty smart. For an American dude, anyway."

Then they gave each other a high five. I just rolled my eyes at them. At least they were now acting like six-year-olds instead of four-year-olds.

"AH . . . ACHOO!" Chloe fake sneezed. "Nikki, you don't want the rest of these pastries, do you? I just accidentally sneezed on them! Sorry!"

"I love happy endings!" Zoey gushed. "Who's up for a group hug?!"

Zoey, André, Chloe, Brandon, and I all huddled into a big group hug while Tiffany and MacKenzie brooded behind us.

"This whole thing was YOUR stupid idea!" Tiffany complained. "And now my summer is RUINED!"

"No, it was YOUR stupid idea!" MacKenzie grumbled. "You're the one who's obsessed with posting SELFIES on social media!"

"Well, get used to it, girlfriend! We'll BOTH be taking A LOT of selfies together this summer when we're FORCED to volunteer at the senior citizens center!" Tiffany shot back.

Tiffany and MacKenzie totally DESERVE each other.

In spite of all their mean girl drama, I managed to survive my Not-So-Secret Crush Catastrophe!

OMG! I've been in here writing for so long, I'm late for bio!

I gotta go!!

☺!!

Today was the last day of school!

SQUEEEE ☺!!

Which means that my SUMMER VACATION has officially started!

Brandon came over to give Daisy another doggie obedience lesson. I think they're really helping, and I've noticed a drastic improvement in her behavior lately.

Today was a socialization session for Daisy so she could learn to get along with other dogs.

Brandon brought over three dogs from Fuzzy Friends to hang out with her.

But, unfortunately, Brandon and I got a little distracted. I think WE probably did MORE SOCIALIZING than the DOGS did. . . .

497

499

Now that I think about it, maybe Daisy's lessons HAVEN'T really helped her that much. Hmm . . . maybe she needs MORE lessons. Like EVERY DAY. I'll mention that to Brandon ☺!!

I still haven't made a final decision about the Bad Boyz tour and the trip to Paris.

Zoey and Brandon say I should definitely go to Paris because I love art and it will be a life-changing experience!

Chloe and André say I'd be CRAZY not to go on tour because it'll be a BLAST and Paris will be there . . . FOREVER!

I'm not sure WHAT I'm going to do. Maybe I should try to do BOTH?! Because sometimes you gotta be a BEAUTY and a BEAST! Sorry! I can't help it. . . .

I'M SUCH A DORK!!

☺!!

PUPPY LOVE ☺!!

Go online fo

Visit the **Dork** Diaries webpage
www. **DORK**diaries.co.uk

Read Nikki's secret blog and ask her questions

Submit your own DORK DIARIES fan artwork and videos

"Dork Yourself" widget that lets you create your own Dork cartoon

Exclusive news and gossip!

Download a DORK DIARIES party pack!

Fabulous competitions and giveaways

more dorky fun!

Now you can find DORK DIARIES on Facebook and twitter too!

connect with other fans of the series!

Rachel Renée Russell is the #1

New York Times bestselling author of the block-buster book series Dork Diaries and the bestselling series The Misadventures of Max Crumbly.

There are more than forty-five million copies of her books in print worldwide, and they have been translated into thirty-seven languages.

She enjoys working with her daughter Nikki, who helps illustrate her books.

Rachel's message is "Always let your inner dork shine through!"